L'Excisée

L'Excisée

by
**Evelyne
Accad**

Translated from the
French
by David K. Bruner

Three Continents Press
Washington, DC

©David K. Bruner 1989

First English Language Edition

Three Continents Press
1901 Pennsylvania Avenue, N.W.
Washington, D.C. 20006

First published as L'Excisée
L'Harmattan, 1982

Library of Congress Cataloging-in-Publication Data:

Accad, Evelyne.
    [Excisée. English]
    L'Excisée/by Evelyne Accad: translated from the French by David
K. Bruner.—First English language ed.
        p.   cm.
    ISBN 0-89410-596-5
    ISBN 0-89410-597-3 (pbk.)
    I. Title.
PQ3989.2.A325E9213   1989
        843-dc20   89-5014
                                                                CIP

Cover art and illustration by Max Winkler
©Three Continents Press 1989

Translator's Dedication

This translation I dedicate to my wife, Charlotte—my beloved and invaluable partner in bringing attention to contemporary women writers from various parts of the world, writers of whom American readers are, as yet, insufficiently aware.

Author's Dedication

For Jay Zerbe

For Monique Loubet

Translator's Preface

A book like *L'Excisée* is under a handicap even before it is written. The subject matter facts are ones which most readers—even some otherwise impartial and open-minded ones—prefer to deny rather than to recognize. Female circumcision (excision, rather, for one is speaking of the removal of the clitoris, and the labia major and minor) is ugly to contemplate. The stupid brutality of the ritual procedure upon very small and terrified little girls shocks one's better instincts. So, denial is an easy defense. "It is no longer done," one is told. I, indeed, was told just that in January 1986 by a guide to the Cairo Museum. However, as I visited with Nawal El Saadawi a few days later, I was able to confirm a quite opposite truth. There have been some changes in sophisticated, metropolitan areas, perhaps, but little change elsewhere. The woman behind the veil is excised physically (really mutilated), but has also had cut from her the power to learn, to love, to choose, to participate as a full human being in a world still governed by men who think *macho* is bravery, rather than the anti-intellectual cowardice it truly is. (The macho conveniently forgets that he depends upon his *gang* for his justification and support and upon his frail victims for sure, safe victories.)

L'Excisée knows all this and it deals quite unabashedly with it. It is remarkable, however, that it—and its central character, E. (like its author Evelyne) are seeking justice, love, and beauty; never revenge or battle victory. It is a book written in the spirit of affirmation, rather than

1

denial. If its heroine is destroyed, like a modern Ophelia, it is not because of innate fault or anger. She is capable of suffering and being broken only because she is loving and honest.

The prose of *L'Excisée* is everywhere poetic, poetic in simple, non-ornate ways. And within the "prose" there are interspersions of verse, a kind of folk verse, though it is created by the writer, who, in her own actual life does compose and sing, to her own guitar's accompaniment, poems like those in the fiction. Indeed, Evelyne has often sung to women in hospitals, sufferers of the kinds of atrocious customs *L'Excisée* has chosen to deal with.

The reader who demands strict form and structure or who is unhappy in the face of simple repetitions and shifting points of view, or who cannot be at ease when sentiments are stated artlessly and openly will find *L'Excisée* hard to assimilate. But, to all other readers, it offers an honest and a clean breath of life-giving hope. For one easily discovers that "excisions" of various kinds and degrees, arising also from dogmas other than Islamic ones, are basic to hatreds and wars and the needless uglinesses of human behavior. "To do better and to be better is within our power" is the credo of *L'Excisée*.

David Bruner
Ames, Iowa
July, 1987

When the dragon saw that he had been cast down upon the earth, he pursued the woman who had given birth to a male child. And the two wings of the great eagle were given to the woman so that she might flee to the desert, to her abode where once, ages since, she was nurtured the better part of her days far from the serpent's face. Then, from its mouth the serpent poured forth water as a flood behind the woman in order to draw her along by that stream. But the land gave succor to the woman and it opened its mouth and swallowed the flood the dragon had cast forth from its mouth. And the dragon was angered against the woman and it drew itself away to war against the others of her issue, against those who keep the commandments of God and bear the witness of Jesus. And it stationed itself upon the sands of the sea.

> And the woman takes the child and runs
> She runs and runs toward the sea
> She has enfolded the child in her veil
> To protect it against the sands and the sun
> And the child clings to the woman
> And the woman stumbles in the sand
> The sun is quite low and the sea far away
> And the woman fears lest she reach it not

The summer has been hot, a summer of dust and madness, a summer of fury, humid as the tears of a child in pain, bitter as a green hazel nut. Everywhere armed bands have beseiged Beirut, stirring hate, sowing fear, breaking trusts, crushing spirits. Barricades have risen in the streets themselves, under that same sky, in that same city: brother against brother, sister against sister, children drawn into the debacle. The canons, the machine guns, the rockets and the rifles have rumbled from Christian side and from Muslim side, tearing the silence, creating desolation, perforating hope. Blood has run, a black blood laden with lineage, an ignominious blood, a vengeful blood. Corpses scattered upon the streets cause panic, call out for other deaths. The sea has reddened, then turned to ink, at length swallowing its shame.

The President has made a speech, stressing the urgency of the moment, the need to end these battles, to begin negotiations, to sit down before a cup of coffee and learn who began it all and why. Leaders of various groups have smiled and scratched their heads at the naiveté of the President. The shooting has been stopped for a while, allowing everyone to rearm, to quickly bury the dead, and to plan new offensives.

And the battles have begun again, greater and more violent because more vengeful; more mortal because nourished by the dead. Stray pedestrians are stopped, questioned, and depending upon their religious denominations, summarily executed, coldly and upon the spot, sometimes behind the tree, sometimes in a ditch, but more often against a wall, their arms crossed; they will never know why they were slain. Houses at strategic places are occupied, enormous canons filling the windows; other houses are also occupied, their inhabitants' throats slit. No one bothers about the skies which wear mourning of black smoke: opaque veils always drawn, veils with a sharp odor which stifles, strangles, suffocates.

The Sixth Fleet has received orders to steam towards the eastern Mediterranean. America and Russia are on the alert. America wants national integrity granted to a small nation which protects her guns and butter. Russia is not content to have the Sixth Fleet at her doorsteps. She claims that America has no intention of safe-guarding an integrity, but rather, wants to question all integrities and to appropriate them to herself. The Security Council has assembled to discuss Lebanese problems. There is a vote which calls for a cease-fire. All members vote aye, except for Russia which abstains. The leaders of the armed bands smile and scratch their heads. They will again have failed at a cup of coffee and a discussion. They will again have had time to rearm and bury the dead.

The second truce is followed by battles and terrible massacres, above all in the mountains. For years, the villagers have felt the storm coming, just as they feel whether rain will or will not come to water their fields, whether the wind from the desert will proclaim itself with withered flowers, a sick beast, a star that fails to shine on a summer night. Even the villagers themselves, have learned to be distrustful, to arm themselves, to group together according to their denominations. The Lebanese villager is proud. He has a sense of honor sharpened by centuries of resistance to whatever he does not want; he has it from centuries of withdrawal into the mountains fleeing persecutions, escaping domination. His sense of honor is translated into the preservation of the virginity of his daughters and the respectibility of his wives and the avenging of blood by blood. To provoke a villager is to rush into a sure and certain fate. Battles in the mountains are atrocious and passionate.

In town, on the plains and in the mountains, each person counts his dead and cries out his anguish. Groups to take action through non-violence are formed. They march through the streets riddled with bullets, below houses battered down like stacks of cards: Catholic, Orthodox, and Maronite priests; Sunni, Shiite and Druz sheikhs; Protestant pastors and Jewish rabbis all hold hands crying out against the carnage, wishing to refuse it the names of their religious identities. But, this is not a war of religion or religious identifications. They have forgotten the masses who rot in misery and who seek to burst through the roofs of their putrid hovels. They have forgotten that those who beg their bread are not loved. They withdraw as they have ventured forth, a body of people, moving, peace-loving—refreshing in times of fever. Many are struck down and arise again to give blessing, only to be struck down anew. Many die without ever having truly understood. Women weep and raise their arms to heaven, imploring God to take pity. Their tears run even to the sea, which seems to expect them.

An ending, an ending seems to approach with the end of summer. The conflicts quiet down, little by little, without one's ever knowing why or how. There is even a new President who has been elected. There is even a new regime in Iran. There is even a smiling America whose white and blond G.I.'s excite the harbor girls and the school girls who have escaped the traditional surveillance. There is even a rain which has begun to fall, piercing the clouds of smoke, rending the shadows, renewing the sea. There is now all this. But no one understands. Where is the hatred which was unleashed all summer? Where is the lightning which struck down, which terrorized, which shattered all basic values? Where is the answer to the why of this war? Silence slowly establishes itself, a silence empty and cold, cruel as a rapier.

Fear settles in at the base of the heart, and no one dares talk, no one dares ask questions. It is definitely the end of summer.

O, women, may you be in like manner, submissive to your husbands, so that if some of them are not affected by words, they may be won over by the behavior of their wives, seeing your habit of living chastely and modestly. Cleave not to that external adornment which consists of plaited hair, golden ornaments, or the garments one wears, but rather, to the internal adornment hidden in the heart: the incorruptible purity of a sweet and passive spirit, which is of great worth before God. Thus were former saintly women clothed who trusted in God, submissive to their husbands, like Sarah who obeyed Abraham and called him her lord. It is of her that you became the daughters in doing what is good, without letting yourselves be bothered by any fear.

Husbands, show you, in turn, wisdom in dealing with your wives, as with a weaker sex; honor them in like manner to inherit with you the blessings of life.

> Around the sea there is a wall
> And the woman strikes and scratches it, making raw
> her hands
> The child has fallen in the sand and it cries.

Instruct the believing women that they lower their glances, that they be chaste, that they permit to be seen of themselves only that which covers them, that they draw their veils back against their bosoms; that they show themselves in their individual costumes only to their husbands, or to their husbands' sons, or to their sisters' sons and their wives, or to their slaves or male servants who are unable to have carnal desire, or to the young boys who are not yet knowing of the form of woman. Instruct these believing women that they never put foot to earth in a way to show the charms they hide. Come to Allah, all you believing men. You may well be blessed.

The serpent has drawn near the child.

E. walks along her street, with a step a bit reticent, a bit intimidated. School has just reopened its doors after a long delay due to the public events. She has changed schools to avoid crossing a city riddled by bullets and stones hurled at random. In place of the French school, it will be the English school this year. In place of the influence of French

6

culture, there will be an American substitute. In place of Charlemagne and Napolean, she will ingest Coca-cola and rock-and-roll. E. carries in her hands her school books and a ball-point pen.

The street movements have just begun, as they have begun every day since the end of the struggles, just as if nothing had happened, as if the street had never seen dead bodies, as if a child had never cried out at this very spot at the crossroads. It is there that the petty fruit and vegetable merchants call out the prices of their wares and that the housekeepers choose among the market carts, discuss prices, pretending to be unable to find this or that item quite to their taste—in order to get a better bargain.

E.'s attention is internal and not upon these customary noises, so incongruous after those of the summer past. For here is an Evangelist tent, just set up in her quarter, hurling appeals to salvation each evening at the crowd; a tent called a Revival Tent, for it seeks to awaken the conscience to a religious renewal, thinking to be able to transcend hate by love and bridge the distances and differences between opposite camps by means of Christ. Didn't Christ say: I am the Way, the Truth, and the Life. No one comes to the Father except through Me?

But these calls from the tent create a void in E. and a terrible desire to run away, just as do the monotonous lessons of that school from which she has escaped. There has been too much blood. There have been too many dead. There have been too many scattered corpses under a terrifying sunlight. There have been too many camps leveled and children gassed. Too many injustices and useless sufferings accepted on bended knees. How can one accept facile solutions in the face of such miseries? How can one permit the seeds of revolt to die in oneself, which now and then germinate and make a desert bloom? Why crush within oneself the whirl of passion, which illuminates in red again the darkest and most barren corners, and which now and again in hearts and lives which have no more to lose, disinfects the wounds, repairs the injuries, cauterizes the sores?

E. has reached the school. Rima, one of her classmates, takes her aside:

—Listen. A man has been noticing you and following you for several days. He wants to meet you. I told him I'd introduce you. He's going to wait for us outside the school doors.

The tone Rima used stressed that E. ought to feel flattered. Rima and her group were a bunch of girls "on the loose" who listened to Elvis Presley and flirted with the G.I.'s of the Sixth Fleet.

They had a bad reputation in the quarter and most parents forbid their daughters to associate with them. They darkened their eyes with kohl and their eye-shadowed glances sought to please and engage. They showed in their eyes sadness charged with fatal tragedy. They knew that they were "different" and would have to pay for that. They had broken with certain traditions, but they had entered into another system of rules even more violent and more cruel. Codes of honor regulated by family yielded to codes of honor regulated by society. And this latter code never pardons. An eye for an eye, a tooth for a tooth. And where a woman was concerned: two women for one man, two eyes for one eye, two teeth for one tooth. From time to time, one of these girls rebelled, put an end to her days by swallowing poison, or by hurling herself from the height of her balcony. And the newspapers took note of these cripples in "Random Notes" or took no notice of them at all. Once again, a poor hysterical girl in search of an illusion. And if that suicide really was a crime, committed by a brother pressed to cleanse his family honor in blood, everyone applauded. One hailed the victory of the well-oiled code.

The bell rings.

Rima is waiting outside for her. For a minute, E. hoped that Rima would have forgotten. The street is burning hot. The merchants seek shade in the corners of buildings. Children in school smocks return home to eat. From time to time, a taxi honks, a man spits, a woman calls out. The air is suffocatingly hot. E. can hardly breathe. Rima is in a hurry; she draws E. along.

He is there, at the corner, waiting for them. The sunlight, beating down upon his back gives a sharp outline to his silhouette. He advances and E. would like to run away. Rima makes the introductions. The name has sharp resonances which strike her to the heart and which she dares not identify. E. isn't able to look at the man whose stare transfixes her and who seems to divine her very thoughts.

She excuses herself. She is waited for at home. She mustn't be late. There would be trouble. She rushes off precipitately, climbs the stairs two at a time, and arrives all out of breath.

The whole family is at the table, already eating. She begs pardon and takes her place next to her little brother. She lowers her eyes for a blessing. Mama regards her carefully and fills her plate. Papa is occupied with his eating. E. has difficulty swallowing. Suddenly that name recurs to her. That name, that name, it is a Muslim name, mus-ul-man name, as if spelling out syllables in her head would change anything. The gravity of the moment which is already gathering dark clouds above her head. How could Rima? She should know E.'s family.

—Are you coming to pray in the little tent this evening before the meeting? Mama asks.

The blood of Christ washes all your sins away.

8

A white banner carrying these words stretches above the large tent. A crowd of people enter at the open flaps. A fine dust mixed with the bitter odor of sweat hovers in the humid air, but people press together, one against another. Some shake hands. Others embrace. There are women from her church whom she recognizes.They all have covered heads and humble and submissive expressions. She does not want to be like them, not now, not ever. She will never bring a flabby body and a covered head, to smile with ecstacy before the Supreme Being. Never will she allow herself to hold herself bowed down in an attitude of pain and sacrifices.

Papa is already on the platform, alongside of the preacher, as translator. The two men stand up, one wiry, harsh, lean, dressed in black: the Preacher; the other small stout dressed in gray: Papa and Dogma, Papa and System, Papa who knows the Word and can explain it. Papa and Premise. Papa and Preacher. All the P's gathered together to explain, to prod, to probe, to pronounce the Truth: here is the Way, walk upon it. Papa pronouncing the Way—erected, built, shaped in stone. Papa and the Commandments received from Pater-all-Powerful, from Pater Celestial, Papa receiving his orders from the Pater Omniscient, Omnipotent, Omnipresent, from the divine and unexhaustible spring, Papa and Power. Papa and Victory.

They intone a canticle which the crowd takes up with fervor. The man in black begins to preach with fire. His eyes a jet flame. He gesticulates and his hands become now menacing, now appeasing. He wipes away the sweat which drips from his forehead: Golgotha and blood, the crown of thorns and blood. Repent! Accept Christ into your lives and you will find true happiness. Come to Christ, you who are tired and heavy-laden and He will give you rest. Papa also is weltering with heat and appears transported in an ecstasy. I am the Voice crying in the wilderness. Repent before even more terrible times arrive. In these coming times, there will be so much suffering and so much distress, that you shall call to the mountains: fall upon us; and to the rivers: draw us under.

The city will be purified by blood. And the child will lead the lion the lamb into green pastures. For His name's sake. And the lion, the lamb, and the serpent will feed peacefully side by side. And he who has believed shall be led by Christ to miraculous springs where he shall receive a crown of pure gold. In His name's sake. For He shall have triumphed over evil. And there shall be no more wars and there shall be no more hates for the dragon will have been manacled for a thousand years. A thousand years of peace on earth. There shall be no more hunger and no more cruelties, and all who have believed will reign with Him and with the Child. And all those who have triumphed will walk in

9

green pastures in company with the Child, the lion, the lamb, and the serpent.

The people come forward en masse, responding to the plea for a change in their ways. They want so much to have a new formula to help them support their daily lives, a remedy for their miseries. Among them are both great and small, both men and women, both children and elderly.

They file down the aisles, a crowd stirred up, as if drawn to a miraculous spring, a delirious crowd lifted above the banality of daily life, above its shabbiness, a crowd drawn towards the love which passeth all understanding.

Lamb of God, I come I come. Christ has said: I am the Resurrection, the Truth, and the Life. No one comes to the father but by Me.

There are some who cry, others who pray, others whose eyes are turned towards the heavens in an attitude of supplication. E. looks at Papa and Mama. Both are praying. She sees one of her brothers who is moving forward with the crowd of the redeemed. She feels remorse. Is she really so separated from them all? Shouldn't she, as well, arise and march towards her redemption; wouldn't that be in accord with the principles which "they" have inculcated in her from the cradle on? Why can she not do it? What is it which holds her back? Is she so different, and why?

Yet the crowd is gentle and enticing. Only one more step to take and she will be snatched up in the crowd. All her problems will have an answer. She will go with fortitude to her eternal rest. But, does she want this answer, this rest? She likes to feel within herself the contradictions which disturb, the questions which tear her apart, the awareness that she exists because she is a responsible being. She doesn't want to die, to die in her very soul now before having lived, before having understood the whys of these agitations which arouse her, which torment her. Anguish itself is preferable to the abnegation of oneself. Even suffering is better than renunciation.

The agitation ceases. She feels relieved. But there is a clutching at her throat. She rushes outside hoping to get away from the crowd. Outside, it has begun to rain. The day's heat is swept away, the air cleared. She feels a desire to drink that water charged with the dust and dirt of the city. She would like to run long and far in that healing and substantial rain, even yet impregnated with the warmth of the day.

And when the prophecies will have been fulfilled (seven days times seven), the skies will open, the clouds will rend apart. And He will appear on high in all His Glory. The sunlight will spread itself upon the earth. Springs will burst forth and rivers infinite shall flow. The very heart of the earth shall split into a thousand clusters, into a thousand lights, into a thousand fluids, into a thousand serums of life fibers of love woven into a will to comprehend, into the will to develop, into the will to make triumph the forces of life, and of tenderness, and of love. And the little child will lead them into the light where they will overcome evil, and war, and the forces of power, of destruction, and of death.

We are comfortable, sheltered in our houses, in our rooms which smell of freshly ironed linen, of soap-scrubbed floor tiles, of furniture and doors well polished. Outdoors, the tempest rages. A dog howls somewhere, a machine-gun sputters somewhere else, and the child abandoned in the tent weeps and cries out. The South is divided, fueled by both sides along the sea, and its waves roll out upon a shore of blood and shame. The bird glides and falls in the heaviness of a wind bitter and filled with canon-dust and hatred.

Girls in uniform play in the school's courtyard; their laughter spreads more strongly than the stuttering of war-planes. E. feels sad, anguished, tormented by contradictory feelings and the fear of having to face the new situation: there in the heart of the new desert, a large flower has just been planted. It is beautiful but ephemeral, for the desert will triumph over it and the dryness will kill it and a hot, arid breath will carry off its delicate and tender petals. And the wind will blow a sandy dust over all that lives, over all that breathes, over all that seeks to triumph over death. And the union of two beings who love one another will be condemned as something infamous and forbidden. And a love forming between a Christian and a Muslim will be cut at its roots, torn up before it could grow and produce buds and fruits. And the little child will seek in vain a way to the river. The river will have dried up and all its springs dessicated and burned out. And the morning star will be veiled in the smoke of powder and death. And the bird will be asphyxiated, napalmed, turned to ashes.

Rima comes up to her.

—Well? How did you like him?

—How could you? A Muslim . . . He is a Muslim, isn't he?

—Yes. A Palestinian from Jaffa, I believe.

—Oh! Still better!

—Don't you think he looks like James Dean? You could go out with him in a group, with others. It's the same way with me—my parents won't let me go out alone with my friend. You've got to know how to work it.

Rima, a young, emancipated Arab woman who knew how to work it, who found alternate routes, crooked roads. A young, Arab woman who swooned over everything American, over the American male as if he were a god, a young, blond god like James Dean: coarse mouth, sensual look, suicidal life-style, heroics in the service of a consumer society, a young Christ crucified for cans of processed food. James Dean-Muslim-Palestinian of Jaffa, an impossible mixture but desired by Rima. America gobbling up Palestine and spewing her forth after being well stuffed, after having sucked out her life's sap. And Rima, the Unaware, drawn towards all the Dean-Presley-Graham-York-Coke-

Rock-Doll-Sex-Machine-Roll, and dancing, dancing, dancing out of breath and kneeling before the Statue of Liberty, lips pressed against the cold marble, thanking God for the gift of grace, for having chosen America to make triumph His Word and His Church, for having chosen America to make triumph the Salvation and the Redemption, life in a Jesus-Christ-Dollar, for making live there the segregationist churches, the churches KKK, the churches Texaco, the churches IBM, the churches Xerox, the churches Ford, the churches Polaroid, and the churches Exxon.

And Rima does not understand at all. E. would never be allowed to go out, alone or accompanied. On rare occasions, she had gone to the homes of classmates for birthday parties. She had always felt plainly, badly dressed in front of her stylish classmates who sparkled in their most lovely gowns. She had fled from these affairs, which brought her only a kind of bitterness at the gaudy show of wealth on display. Once, she had overheard a comment which greatly wounded her:

—How ridiculously dressed that daughter of the missionaries is! What utter vulgarity, really . . .

Silently, she had returned the insult. They were the vulgar ones, these families who had built there fortunes on the backs of the poor who squatted in misery in quarters only two paces from their wainscoted villas! These bourgeois Lebanese families and these daughters of "good families" who attended the French school out of snobbery, to learn to speak "the French of France," to dress "à la Parisienne." She scorned their ribbons of rose satin tying back their silky braids, their cakes and canapés from the Swiss bakeshop, "The Bourgoisie," and the blatant display of their life of ease.

At the end of the class at noon, he is waiting for her. Has he come for Rima or one of her group? No, it is towards E. that he moves with that somewhat mocking smile she has already noted about him. In the background, other girls whisper and watch with envy a blond Muslim with blue eyes—a Palestinian god, a blond with blue eyes, James Dean reincarnate, the American idol—and all the young, enraptured, delirious Lebanese and all the emancipated, young Arabs dancing Rock 'n' Roll to the light of an Elvis Torch, wriggling and fidgeting. And America taking over Palestine with blondness, the blond of grain, the blond of bread, the blond evoked by the corner beggar as a talisman, as a miraculous elixir: "for your blue eyes, Oh my blond one, may God make you fecund." That Arab rejection of blackness. *Black Skin White Masks*. The darkness of grain, the darkness of bread, the bread of bread.

the bread of renewal
the bread of hope
the bread of life.

He draws her along the streets saturated with the sunlight of midday. He wants to see her again. He wants her to invent pretexts at home to see him, so that they may pass some time together. His looks are tender, the appeal of his eyes irresistible. It is the Palestinian of hope, the blue of the sea regained, flowers of a world recaptured, trees of an irrigated desert. Grapes crushed and juice-giving.

Wine flowing in the blood
the blood of shame
the blood of hate
vision which emerges in spite of steel and spilled blood.

But E. does not wish to have to lie to her family. She refuses to see him. She says no to that hope which has sprung up for she does not like lies, crooked ways, things which must be hidden, the need to manipulate . . . I, I wish to be upright.

—I don't want to lie, deceive, hide.

—Ah, you don't like to lie! You are conservative! I like that very much in you. But I am patient. I can wait.

The whole family is already at the table when she comes in. It is Wednesday and the aunt whom she loves very much is there. Mama is looking at her fixedly. Does she guess something? Already Papa is questioning her.

—You're quite late. What were you doing?

—The teacher had to explain a problem for us.

The first lie, which burns her mouth, but passes her lips so quickly, nonetheless. The first slash into her protected, nurtured, encircled soul. "I had to, I had to," she tells herself. And she looks down at her soup to avoid seeing the effect of her lie on Papa's face.

Woman against the wall. Woman who tricks in order to live. Woman who compromises herself to live. Woman who pierces the wall with a pin to see the other side of her prison, the side of liberty, the side of space. Woman who works slowly, patiently, in order to breathe, in order not to suffocate, in order to find the space again which leads to the sea and to the infinite waves.

—I brought a book to read to you, says Aunt. *In Search of El Dorado.* The story of the Huguenot martyrs in France. There were even children ready to be burned alive rather than deny the true Gospel.

From E.'s tender childhood on, Aunt has read them such stories, nourishing them as if the stories were milk from her breast. Aunt has a voice both sweet and taking. The stories are often captivating, stories from far away in dreamed-of lands, from lands full of child-heroes who without a word—or while chanting triumphant canticles—let themselves be devoured by lions or be burned alive. Papa and Mama often told her that these times of persecution could come again and that it is necessary to be ready to die, rather than deny the Faith. E. likes to think of the sweetness of dying in heroic grandeur. How would she receive the bite of flames, the tearing of fangs? Sometimes she burns herself in order to know the cruelty of the act, the profundity of stoicism. And the voice draws her far away, very far, towards a heaven partly opened to which angels with bright, golden wings come bearing the charred children and who bathe them with tears which are a thousand precious stones. All the chosen are taken along the street of pure gold which leads to a resplendant, eternal palace. Other angels sound the trumpets and cymbals and sing hymns of victory. Each soul who has triumphed receives a white robe and a crown of gold and precious stones. And the voice transforms these crowns into ribbons of rose satin, tying back their silky braids, as she has seen on her classmates at the French school. And the angels turn into mothers who bring them babas-au-rhum from The Bourgeoisie.

The music changes into the national anthem. E.'s head whirls with all sorts of things. But the voice implores. In the palace there is the throne of the Lamb. The Lamb is Christ, and He looks at her, thanking her for having suffered for him. But Christ turns into the Palestinian Muslim. A Palestinian Muslim from Jaffa does not belong in El Dorado! A Palestinian Muslim from Jaffa does not belong to the elect! A Palestinian Muslim from Jaffa is not a lamb!

The message from the tent this evening is strong, direct, luminous as a star made of the steel of the prayers of the elect.

But for those who have rejected Him, He keeps a fiery furnace.

The city is in flames. The city burns, writhing with fear, encircled with barbed wire. The little child is blind and gropes its way towards the river. Its hands are torn by thorns. The stars are dark, consumed by flames of hate.

And the woman seeks a way out
The woman brushes patiently aside the stone which strikes
her
The woman enfolds in her arms a dead child
The city lies slain beneath the ashes.

The preacher pictures a flight over the ocean in a plane of flames, when he and his family were about to perish. They no longer had any hope. It was a prayer and faith which saved them. The sinner is like the passenger caught in a burning plane. For the world and its greed there is perdition. Only prayer can save it. Only Christ can deliver it and snatch it from the fiery furnace, from eternal death.

But she wishes to cry out against the Injustice which metes out its own idea of justice to all of Palestine paralyzed under Authority, under the forces of Power, the forces of Progress, and the forces of Propaganda.

> She cries out for the women sewn into their tents
> the women mutilated in their gardens.
> Palestine beaten down
> And the bird dead at the crossing of paths

Aunt also seems to suffocate and asks E. to take her to a taxi. E. guides Aunt across the boulevard. In the crowd E. feels a look fixed insistently upon her, the Palestinian's look. It is an entire world which permeates her. It is an entire world which seeks to attach itself to her. It is a world to which she wishes to open herself, which she wishes to understand. The wide world calls to her, the unknown beckons.

Aunt kisses her and steps into the taxi. Immediately the cab moves along while Aunt waves her hand. Suddenly he stands before her with his mocking smile:

—I was in the tent this evening. I wanted to see you. I almost became a convert so your father would accept me.

—If you convert *for* something, it is no conversion.

—I was kidding. I have no intention of converting. I don't believe in religions. They merely serve to create gulfs between human beings, between peoples. But, for me, the Muslim religion—it is a kind of necessary code of national conscience. Consider a bit: it's what helps the Algerians fight at this very moment. It's what gives them a unity, a strength they need—without which they would be nothing. When one has been driven from one's country, as I have been, one takes more cognizance of one's own people, which, unfortunately, is mixed up with religion.

—But Christianity is also an Arab religion.

—Not for me.

He hardened, became intransigent, peremptory. He became an unknown who frightened her. They approached her house and she signalled goodbye to him. Before turning away, he drew her to him and kissed her passionately on the mouth. A kiss of tenderness and of possession. A kiss wished-for, and repulsed. A man sure of himself, of his power, of his strength. Man penetrating woman to assure himself of his power, of his strength. Man penetrating woman to assure himself that he is Master, that he is the inventor of gardens, of plains, of harvests.

Palestine-Woman
Palestine-Garden
Palestine-Child
Palestine of worlds lost and found again.

But to all who have received Him, to those who believe in His name, He has given the power to become children of God.

The words float about the tent, words which seek to trouble, words which seek to fulfill, Biblical words, words millenial which people have heard throughout all time: the power to become children of God, miraculous words, a remedy against misery, a balm against fear.

The fig tree is known by its figs, and the olive tree, by its olives. Thus also, the child of God is known by his fruits. *I hear your words*, says the Amen. I know you are neither cold nor boiling. If only you would be cold or boiling! Thus, since you are luke-warm and neither cold nor boiling, I will vomit you from my mouth. I, I call back and I punish all those whom I love. Have zeal, therefore, and repent. Look now, I stand at the door and I knock. If someone hears my voice and opens the door, I shall enter the house; I shall sup with him and he with me.

Tyre is in flames
Tyre is violated by the man from the South
And the man hammers the earth
And the man guts the dwellings
And the man draws teeth from the woman and plucks out
hair by hair from her.
He cracks the skull of the infant.

And the Word is proclaimed. And the Language of Man is based upon Truth. And historic facts are cited as proofs of Glory, as proofs of Civilization, as proofs of Knowlege, as proofs of Wisdom, as proofs of Progress. And Man brandishes his Phallus-Facts-Jargon as a banner under which one must bend down, which one must accept if one wishes to know truth, if one wishes to create History and imprint the Progress of his Times. And the forces of historic fact and the forces of power and knowledge destroy the forces of tenderness and love and life. And the world shatters in a great atomic holocaust. And Life is destroyed by the Word.

Rima has come over with P. (the Palestinian) to sit near E. Both are whispering and laughing. One of the young persons in charge of the tent approaches E. and asks her to make her friends be quiet. E. signals them to follow her and leaves the tent. All glances converge upon them, heavy looks of disapproval, judging looks, looks shocked and surprised.

—What's the matter? Rima asks.

—The young man was furious because you laughed. He asked me to keep you quiet. I preferred to leave.

—But why didn't he ask us himself?

—Don't forget she's the daughter of the preacher! P. exclaims in a mocking tone.

—I'm going to leave you, says Rima. I only came to accompany him because he was afraid to enter the den of wolves alone. I see he was quite right.

P. takes E. by the hand and they step out into streets still hot from the day's sun. They walk a long while in silence through alleys smelling of fish, of garlic, of frying; they walk along the great boulevards of the Grotto of Pigeons animated with a thousand lights, with braying taxis, with taxi drivers who swear or spit, with idlers seated at tables enjoying the aroma of an ice cream or a coffee, with melodies filtering out from various night clubs—langorous melodies of Um Kalthum who wails a lament, howling a bedevilled Elvis Presley rhythm.

> Only yesterday, alleys cut off by crusader barricades
> By crosses
> By the dust from canons, bombs, and the fires of vengeance
> Boulevards sheeted with blood, strewn with corpses
> Grottos of Pigeons, of pigeons flown off, terrorized
> Grotto overhanging a cruel and impassible sea
> Pigeons hunted, pursued, carbonized
> Passersby witnesses of drawings and quarterings, of hangings, closing their eyes, slipping into unknowing.
> And Unknowing closing its eyes for Oblivion.
> Melodies which ought to have been sung, and turned into appeals, into a pang of conscience, into a changing of life, into an enjoyment of the will and the wish to transform society.

The air becomes more and more humid and dirty as they approach the sea. Silence enshrouds them, a silence-accomplice and protector; in spite of codes, in spite of honor systems, and in spite of prohibitions against union between different religious denominations; a silence which bears them above the times, above the troubles, above conventions, above the rage of swords and machine guns, above a civil war filtering in everywhere and engaging more and more quickly all the families of the population, above even the dead birds slain above the clouds.

They sit upon a rock overhanging the cliff. Below, far away, E. views the sea which comes in with soft and regular sound to break upon the shore, a sound of healing.

Sea forever begun anew
Sea laving the rocks of blood
Sea of hope and return
Sea watered with words and tears and wishes
Sea which renews the times
Sea which bears away tired and fallen bodies.

He holds onto her hand, which he caresses softly. A feeling of well-being and freedom rises and unfolds within her like a wave of tenderness and hope. She begins to speak, to express her joy:

—I would love to be like that sea, free to go where I wish, to do what I wish, free to roar, free to foam, free to be calm. Oh, to escape all systems, to exist with the infinite. To return only to the skies, to find myself in the blue, to become eternal, immortal; but not for another system, a system of angels and streets of gold, white garments and song. . . . just to live infinitely without systems, to bury myself in you, join myself with you, know you, know Palestine, banish hates through a bond of true love, a love based upon our mutual understanding, upon tenderness and confidence . . . then to disappear into that sea, never to return, never to know that such a union could not be, such a bond, like all which is truly beautiful, could not last.

—You have taken me by surprise this evening. You have shown an astonishing courage: thus to brave the whole world. I just knew there was a bond between us which would overcome all difficulties. Together we shall rebuild the world, together we shall brave all obstacles, we shall cross the gulfs between out cultures and we shall find compromise. I don't like compromises, but it is necessary, and with you I feel it is possible for our goals are the same. Together we will work towards Palestine.

—But what is Palestine? A goal, children, a love, a country, a mirage, a war, a peace, a common work, a symbol, a word upon which to build a world, an accord upon which to build our life?

—It would take too long for me to explain it all to you. Palestine is for me something precise and one day I shall explain it all to

19

you. Now it's late; it's best that we go back.

He has become withdrawn, sad, taciturn. She does not know why, but she is frightened, frightened by the new feeling she had felt near the waves and frightened of him who has suddenly become an outsider, frightened by that bitter wound she perceives in him, frightened at her own innocence, her powerlessness to understand life, to know the heart of things, alone to teach herself to know, to comprehend, to know herself. They retrace their path in heavy, stormy silence. He no longer holds her by the hand.

> The earth is torn
> The earth is broken
> The earth trembles
> The earth trembles like a drunken man
> She shudders like a shanty
> Her transgression weighs upon her
> She falls and does not rise again
> The earth blares in a great atomic holocaust
> The earth is battered by the murdering forces of
> Man
> She bows beneath the Words of the Phallus-Language
> The earth dies, strangled by Man
> And the child seeks vainly for the flow of the river
> And the child seeks vainly the nourishing breast
> And the child seeks vainly the hand which comforts and
> gives.
> All routes are cut off. All paths are blocked. All roads are
> without exit.

E. regards his profile which is hard and locked. At the corner of a street, adjacent to her own, she stops and asks that he not walk further with her. E. notes his step: a bit nonchalant and heavy. His weight seems to lie heavy upon the soles of his feet and within his back. She feels very sad and overwhelmed. She fears to face her parents. What is she going to tell them? It would almost be better to go back towards the sea and sleep in the salty air with the roar of the waves, curled up on the sand among the seaweed brought in from afar, to forget that she ever existed, to forget that a Palestine exists and that she possesses a secret closed in a case, double-locked—a secret which she might never know.

—Then I saw in the right hand of that one who was sitting upon the throne a book written within and without, sealed with seven seals. And I saw a powerful angel who cried out in a loud voice: 'Who is worthy to open the book and break the seals?' And no one in heaven nor on earth could open the book nor look into it. And I cried that no one was found worthy to open it nor look into it. And one of the old men spoke to me: 'Don't weep, here is the lion of the tribe of Judah; the offspring of David has succeded in opening the book and its seven seals.'

E. no longer fears. She knows she will triumph. She knows that the forces of love and truth and tenderness will mingle within her the fluids, the fibers, the blood, red and warm, the cells filled with milk, the membranes filled with flesh and organs, and these forces will transform them into life—into the powerful brilliance of Life, of Resurrection, and of Creation.

As she mounts the stairs, she hears Papa's voice saying in a menacing tone:

—. . . too much freedom . . . she needs to be restrained.

It would be better to retrace her steps. She has known Papa's belt— leather, heavy— which more than once has whipped about her, leaving violet lines, blacks and blues on her skin, and for reasons less grave than those of the present. But it is already too late. Mama has heard her footsteps and now opens the door, looks at her with reproach. E. stiffens in an attitude of defiance. Why should she be afraid of them? It is now or never for her to triumph, to win and be worthy of Palestine, to vanquish—to uncover the secret too well-wrapped which fills her with curiosity and hope.

—This is what the Holy One, the True One says, He who has the key of David, He who opens and no one will close, He who closes and no one will open: 'I know all your acts. Behold, because you have little power and yet have kept my word and have not denied my name, I have placed before you an open door which no one may close . . . for that one who enters I shall make into a pillar of the temple of my God and he will never more depart; I shall inscribe upon him the name of my God and the name of the City of God, of the New Jerusalem which comes from heaven according to God and my new name.'

Papa is no longer in the room. He has gone to his own room. His absence foretells a storm. It is the silence of violence, the silence of power, the silence of domination and reduction to submission and dependency. It is the triumph of silence from Authority.

—Where were you? Mama asks.

E. dares to reply:

—I was with some friends who were in the tent.

—Were these the friends who failed to show respect during the sermon? Someone came to tell your father that his daughter was laughing with her friends,while he was preaching. It's quite necessary that you explain yourself to him, for he is very angry.

21

—But I haven't anything to explain. I didn't do anything wrong or disrespectful. Someone has lied about me, that's what.

It surely was that little church-saint who had gone to report the behavior of her friends to Papa. How she detested that hypocrisy and those airs of supplication. How far from all of them she was, far from their meanness and their postures of self-righteousness! They were like the Pharisees whom Christ condemned. They were worse than the Pharisees for they preached the message of Christ himself, a message of forgiveness and love, whereas the Pharisees identified themselves with the law—the law of Moses and the Old Testament!

—May all be animated with the same thoughts and the same feelings, full of brotherly love, of compassion, of humility. Do not return evil for evil or abuse for abuse, quite to the contrary, give out your blessings, for it is what you have been called to do to receive your own benediction. Bless those who revile you. Turn the other cheek toward him who strikes it.'

Mama is asking her to do just that, to humble herself to accept her cross in silence, to turn the other cheek, to make an effort to dissipate the atmosphere of misunderstanding and antagonism, so that Papa may be appeased, so that harmony may rule once more in the house.

She knows that Mama is sincere and that it is Mama in the end who will suffer most if she does not explain herself at once. For Papa will make Mama know by a thousand barbs that it is her fault if their daughter has this attitude of revolt and disobedience, if the bad seed has developed in the midst of good crops, if birds of prey fly over the harvest fields, if the turtle doves may no more find their nest, if all of the doves of the land are stolen by the gross, squat neighbor who plies his sport each day, perched on the roof of his house calling them, attracting them with the banner he makes flutter in the wind. It will be Mama who suffers the most and E. cannot allow that to be.

E. approaches Papa's room and knocks at its door.

—Enter, says the Voice.

A tone of command, a tone of Master to slave, a tone shaking the walls of the house, a tone which one dare not contend with, a tone under which one must bow down if one does not wish to see the house crumble, the windows fly loudly apart, a tone which takes away one's spirit because Papa believes he is the protector, sanctifier, fructifier!

E. takes her courage into both hands and enters. Papa is stretched out on the bed, a newspaper in his hands, a horizontal force ready to leap, a screen shielding the holocaust, the prelude to the sacrifice, the inevitable confrontation. He doesn't even raise his eyelids. The silence is icy. She must break the time-stop. She must not just accept the downfall of Palestine. There have been too many bowed backs, trembling brows. There have been too many who have accepted exile through fear and with sacrifice. There has been too much blood spilled in shame and renunciation.

—Mama told me that you were angry because you thought I had laughed in the tent.

—Do you dare to tell me that it is not the truth, and Samuel, a young man most devoted and dedicated to the service of God, would lie to me? And why would he do a thing like that? You are shameless to speak such calumny against a servant of God. Besides, what were you doing outside at this time of day? Didn't you leave the tent in the very middle of the meeting? Tell me, where were you all this time?

—I went out with my friends who were disturbing the service in the tent. But I assure you that I, I was not disturbing it.

—Don't tell me it takes two hours to go out with your friends. You are not only lying, but you are disrespectful as well. I simply won't take that from my daughter, above all now, in a time when we are all working to reawaken the evangelical. I am outraged by your attitude. You truly make me ashamed of you. And who are these friends? What are their names?

Her heart skipped a beat. She had to invent a name, quickly had to say something, invoke Palestine, the batterings, the Cross, the spirit of pardon, anything which . . .

—P. . .

—Ah! Musulman to boot. You choose a fine bunch of friends.

His anger was mounting. She had gone beyond the limits he could tolerate. Now let the lightning strike! Let everything be annihilated! Let everything disappear! Let the flames sweep away all of it! Let the birds fly away forever; let the children fly off above the clouds; let the flies be squashed and the swatters pulverized, all brought down on the spot. There would be no more struggle, no more terror. There would be only the crow of the cock at dawn. There would remain only the cries of the beggar on the empty road. There would remain only her anguish. Papa is red like a poppy. He is going to strike her. She knows it. She ought to run. He is going to batter her, overturn her, make her pass over the sword for pardon, nail her to the wall of lamentation. . . . But what's this? He says nothing; he does nothing. He seems to be calming himself. It is silence, the silence of humiliation, the silence of words which one should understand unsaid, the silence of ransom.

—Go to your room. I do not wish ever to see you again until you have beseeched Him on your knees for forgiveness in shame and tears. And then, it will be necessary that you swear not to speak again with that Musulman. We already have enough difficulties like this, our task is too great to let us be preoccupied with the troubles of P. One day you will understand. One day you will say Papa was right.

She doesn't want any more of that scene which pierces her through like death. She does not want to kneel before injustice, receive the blows of pardon and recovery. She runs to throw herself on her bed and cry with rage. She batters her pillow with her fists to demolish everything. *He'll pay for this!*Someone would pay for it, but not she and P. Oh, that once again there be light, that the clouds fly off and life begin again. She feels a hand on her head. It is Mama who tries to calm her. Mama and her hand of compromise, her hand of reconciliation, her hand which sacrifices everything for others, her hand which lets itself be pierced with the nail so that others may know the Truth.

— You shouldn't cry like that. Come, ask God to help you. You don't recognize that you are entering the jaws of Satan, the enemy of God, the enemy of souls, who seeks to tear us apart as a family because family is a force, a dike against evil which rules throughout the land. Come now, my dear, wipe your tears and ask pardon from God and your papa so that peace may rule once more.

But nothing will stop her revolt, nothing can reconcile her to their ideas. E. no longer wishes to be the child who hides herself to avoid blows, the flower which grows in the shade to avoid the bee, the worm which stays in the cocoon because it is afraid to become a butterfly. She needs room to breathe; she will take it if it isn't given to her.

Mama leaves, bowed, small, sacrificed. It is she who will still bear the brunt of the attack; it is she who will pay ransom. E. hears the voice of Papa, cracking, hard:

—Again! You go to her . . . you console her . . . you are weak with them, that's why they do what they want.

E. leans against the window, head in hands, breathing the air which comes from the street. How lucky that street, that window which looks on the street. It is almost as reassuring as the sea, as the waves against the cliffs, as P.'s hand caressing her own. She feels herself drawn into the street, into the band of students. The bar on the corner with its two red lanterns illuminates the outlines of loitering men.

She sees a shadow stretched out on the building across from her: shoulders somewhat squared, an attitude of nonchalance; that shadow resembles him. It is a shadow which strikes her to the heart, which speaks to her. It is a shadow of hope. It is there where she wishes to take refuge. It is the Palestine of hope. It is everything which makes her heart beat and which transports her into ways of returning to life. She feels stronger, protected by the wings of the shadow, comforted by its presence, by its support, by its appearance.

Mama has reentered. She makes the little brother pray; he is already half asleep, sucking his thumb and smiling at angels. Mama approaches her to make her pray. E. kneels, before the tenderness of Mama, the goodness of Mama, the sweetness of Mama.

—I thank you, my God, for having led our daughter back into the fold. They wish to wrest her from our hands; they wish to wrest her from Thy hands. Do, Thou, extend Thy saving arm and protect all Thy children.

The great heart of Mama, the generosity of Mama, the suffering of Mama who adds:

—And now pray grant her contrition. Pray draw us to Thee for Thy name's sake. Amen.

Mama has a sweet, singing voice. The prayer fills the room. It impregnates the hollow spaces. It makes the walls vibrate. Mama prays with conviction. It is the plain song of her childhood springing forth. It is the eternal peace of salvation which she invokes.

And a miracle is wrought. Mama draws E. toward Papa's room where E. hears herself murmur:

—Pardon.

The promise never to see the young man again is drawn out of her. A promise is sacred. How could she have let herself make it? It was drawn out of her by all the sufferings of Mama, by the sweetness of Mama, by her own chagrin at not being what they would wish her to be. It was drawn out of her because she is frail, with frailty of life; for she does not know how to fight, for she lets her heart speak, her tenderness, her life. It has been drawn out of her because they want nothing of Palestine, because they wish to annihilate those pesky creatures, to relegate them to oblivion, to the bottomless pit from which they will never return.

E. throws herself across her bed and drops off weeping into sleep. She dreams she is on a sea of oil. The nearer she approaches the rocks, the more turbulent the sea becomes. She cries out that she is going to be dashed to bits, that she wishes to go back, that she longs for unction and silence, but no one hears her and the waves draw her on ever more quickly. She feels herself siezed by an engulfing whirlpool.

E. has refused to see him. She has said no to Palestine and to the hope he had permitted her to glimpse. She has said no to the secret they had put together at the shore of the sea. Jesus nailed a second time upon the cross. All Palestine violated a second time. Her horizons shut and veiled without any action on her part. All women veiled, cloistered, beaten, mutilated without revolt, without any acts of aggression or defense.

One day follows another. They are gray and rainy. She has a bitter taste in her mouth, of nightmare, of fear, of defeat. Large violet patches underscore her eyes and she feels a rod in her back which makes every movement difficult. The alley below the house is muddy and full of holes filled with dirty water. She steps over these while thinking of the summer, a trail of horrors and of blood spilled uselessly. Everything is always to begin again. And everything always begins again, always in blood. Enormous bloody puddles all summer have mirrored a storm-changed sky, a sky menacing and gloomy. There will never be any hope. There has been too much blood; there has been too much hate. Too many babes have been crucified. There have been too many old men with mouths agape with fear. Cars blare their horns with impatience; taxi drivers swear and spit more than usual. Why does life always return with the same violence? If only a single cry would resound so that the activity of this street would come to a halt!

There is no one in the schoolyard. The students huddle inside to avoid the rain and cold. Classrooms are humid and somber, their walls gray; the lesson is monotonous and empty. Everything goes on as if nothing had happened that summer, as if nothing had happened yesterday, as if the child had not cried out before dying, as if the little merchant at the corner had not been reduced to mush by a bomb. The geography of the United States stretches out across the black board, a land parceled out and divided, a land united for profit. All the geography of E.'s country wouldn't cover a smidgen of that space. The logic of the strongest. The G.I.'s whom one would find in the harbor. And the songs of Elvis Presley which make the young people of the quarter fidget, but who yesterday held the klashinkof in one hand and the Cross of Christ in the other. Oh, to go far away on a great ship, all alone. To find Palestine again with him, unite with him in Palestine, sieze Palestine for the love of him. To flee from the hypocrisy, the prejudices, the ambiguous smiles and the tyranny of Papa! What good does it do her that the United States is made up of a large number of states united? Haven't they come to divide Palestine, quarter her, massacre her? Have they not gnawed away at her vitality, at the marrow which made her past fruitful and her future open? Chicago extends its tentacles and New York its pincers. Each appropriates what it wants without wanting to feel the consequences of its acts. They are guilty and they make her guilty. When will this unfurling of hatred and of monsters cease? When will this parade of skeletons and blood-suckers stop?

One day Rima proposes an excursion to the Palestinian school where P. teaches. E. with her violin in her hands; today, the conservatory could wait. She hides herself in the back of the car.

E. is in the act of betraying a promise to Papa. She is trampling upon something and it makes her feel sick. But isn't someone always somewhere betrayed and trampled upon? Her very breathing kills something somewhere. Stop her own life? But even that is a betrayal. She refuses to ponder more. She is astonished at the neighborhoods they are traversing, neighborhoods of Druze refugees, neighborhoods whose existence she was unaware of, neighborhoods reeking of misery and hunger. The little streets are narrow and yield up a sour smell. A flock of children in dirty rags, covered with flies walk and play barefooted in the muck. With great, round eyes they watch the vehicle pass.

Then the little streets become dirt paths and one passes by the tiny huts with tanbark roofs to tents pitched almost everywhere. This is one of the camps of Palestinian refugees. Here the wretchedness is frightful; rivulets of dirty water mixed with excrements, wash water, rain water, stale water escaping from tents where entire families live piled one upon another. A girl in a guerrilla uniform, gun on shoulder, mounts guard. P.'s name is spoken. It is a passport. The girl smiles to them and lets them pass. It is the P. of hope which opens doors. It is the P. of reconciliation. A crowd of children, black with filth, stare at the vehicle which covers them with dust, scattering at the same time the flies clinging to their round eyes. Eyes which ask questions without answers. Vehicle breaking the silence of exile. Dust mixed with flies and remorse. Innocence broken even before its birth. How she admires P. who works to make hope be reborn. Somewhere in her heart a chord vibrates. Here salvation is beginning to arise upon the earth and it is P. who works for that salvation. The message of the evangelist tent looks quite vapid alongside of this concrete and vital work. Back home one avoids the tedium and remorse; here one works for life.

The only white cement building, with flat roof and large windows, stands at the end of the path. Heads appear at the corners of the windows. Eyes widely open question. The vehicle, an object of luxury and achievement, parked in a corner, makes the children, who are bunched together in a mass, gape and wonder, eager to take it all in. Brown Palestinian eyes, looks both questioning and tormented; looks of conscience, looks of problems. P. also has a flame shining deep in his eyes, a flame which she returns to him in a blazing cross-communication.

He hadn't quite finished what he was doing, and he made a sign to

the children to go back to their seats and wait till the end of the story:" ...
many years ago in a land called Palestine there lived Samir, a young lad of
Jericho, in the mountains covered with vegetation and acidulous plants,
with birds of warbling song and secure flight. His family wasn't rich, but it
had a well of water ever fresh and pure, a cow giving creamy, rich milk and
some hens whose eggs were large and delicious . . .

"One day—it was June—three black airplanes came flying over the
house—sinister birds, bearers of evil which drove the other birds away.
The next day, the same planes returned to bomb the people. Samir
quickly left the house with his family to hide the mountains. They left
behind them the house, the cattle, and the well—thinking to find them
again after the planes would be gone.

"They came upon the home of an old man whose wife invited them in
to hide. But the planes had followed them. Now the wife had to leave her
husband and escape with them, for the husband was too old and refused to
leave. Samir espied an errant cow. It had gored a child; the blood was
running from the child's head. At nightfall, they stopped under a large
tree. There were birds asleep in its branches. They also fell asleep.

"By morning, the birds had flown away. The skies were covered with
airplanes, black and smoking. Taking the example from the birds which
had fled, the family decided to leave by the roads already burning from
sunlight and from bombs. But Samir wanted to go back to the home of his
childhood. He wanted to see the well again. He was thirsty and wanted to
drink the water of his childhood. He had left a box in his room, a box
containing all his treasure and his secrets. Escaping the attention of his
family, he raced across the mountain. He came near the house and ran to
the well. He wanted to drink water from that well. But a soldier in a
strange uniform barred the way and prevented his approach. Samir
rushed off to the house and tried to enter it, but it was occupied. He was
forbidden entrance. He cried out that there was a box in the room, a box
which belonged to him—to him Samir—a box containing things he held
most dear, but the men struck him and he was obliged to flee again to the
other side of the mountain. He wept bitterly. It seemed to him that he had
left back there a part of his life and his hopes which he would never recover again. He saw the errant cow which had gored a child. He went to
sleep under a tree. In the morning he took flight following the wind. He
reached the frontier of Lebanon which was to become his refuge. He had
nothing to eat or drink for several days. He collapsed from hunger.

"Little by little, among the tents of one of the refugee camps, he moved
in with a family which had taken pity on him. When Samir saw that
Palestine was lost for him and his family, he told himself that the people
should not accept that all was over, they should prepare to fight back.
Samir heard talk about the first contingent of Lion Cubs of the Faith. He

28

joined that camp. There he was trained in the operation of all kinds of arms and other equipment and in the conception and execution of military operations. They created a popular movement in the camp and in the villages. He took courses in Palestine Resistance, in the peoples' war of liberation, in the Chinese and Cuban revolutions, and in Che Guevera. When he became fifteen years old, Samir would participate in the operations directly. Samir had lost his family and his country, but he had rediscovered a sense of dignity, of courage and of brotherhood. He was no longer alone, for all his comrades clasped his hands and they formed an invincible circle."

P.'s voice has become solemn. His hands are stretched out towards the children who regard him intensely, aware of the importance of the movement and the covert appeal of the story. E. also hears it, the appeal of History itself. There is no hesitation. She desires to respond to the enormous thirst for justice which gnaws at her. It is imperative that together they should go to recover the magic box, the box which Samir had to leave behind.

Again they are at the shore of the sea, lying in the sand, clasped together in their dreams. They have left behind the camp and its problems, its children with searching eyes filled with questions. Also they have left behind the city and its heat, its dust and its corpses, its streets choking with blood and hatred.

He makes her party to his plans: to lead her into a desert country where he intends to go the following year to teach.

—I shall carry you off from your family, from your past. Together we shall cross the seas and the sands, together we shall go to the country of my dreams where we shall build a new world, you and I. Together we shall drink water from the well of my childhood and together we shall find again the magic box of my childhood which will help us to achieve that dream, which will teach us how to organize a new nation capable of defending itself, of overcoming and even conquering . . . .

—But I am afraid of battles, I have fear of blood. I am afraid of my family and the harm I may do to them. I fear the city and the people, all those eyes which watch to destroy us: a Muslim and a Christian clinging together on the sands. One kills for less in this country. I am afraid of the great, naked deserts, which are perhaps deprived of the mirages of the water of your childhood. I fear all these things, but I want so to help you realize your dream, for you are my very life. I shall cross the sea and the deserts with you and I shall help you find the box of your childhood.

Their fingers and their lips meld on the sands. The tides lap over them and the breeze caresses them. Sea mews glide low scanning that union developing despite the summer hatreds, despite the mutilated corpses marked with Cross and Crescent, hacked to bits at moonlight, hurled out upon the same sand, carried away into the same sea. Perhaps love will triumph after all. Perhaps love will come to transform the hatreds, the jealousies, the meanness, into hopes, faith and peace. Perhaps love will take these bodies, this blood, these razed camps, these birds, and these calcinated children and from them make a new land of new trees of new fruits, of new beings. She feels herself invaded by faith and peace.

But the tempest broods. The town's armed bands regroup. Shots crack forth a bit here and there. Will they be able to triumph over this new unleasing of hatred? Will love be able to find ways out of this new vicious circle which is being formed and fabricated in the shadows? Will they be able to break down the walls erected around and between them?

At home an unusual silence dominates. Papa is edgy, Mama, silent and turned inward upon herself. Her lips tremble and twitch. She surely must be praying. Papa is preparing for a new journey into Arab lands to preach salvation to Muslims, to convert them and bring them to life eternal. He must feel that something is going on. He looks at her and surveys her. He postpones his departure. He hardly speaks to her. These silences announce a storm and a tempest. She becomes more and more aware that he must know something. These attitudes, these looks, these prayers, these heavy and long meals, these silences are familiar things to her. He is preparing to do something. Something is going to burst out in this house. Something is going to explode in the city. The waiting is agonizing. She draws back more and more into the corners of the house to avoid Papa, to escape meeting his eyes, to not have to see Mama brought to her knees, to no longer feel the menace and the reproaches following her everywhere.

Then one humid and rainy evening when she returned somewhat tardy from the conservatory, blaming the rain and bottle-neck traffic, Papa enters her room with hammer and nails. There is in his movements the determination of the executioner. Sweat beads stand on his forehead, as they do when he preaches. His expression is hard, his voice crushing, his judgement inflexible:

—You have disobeyed us. You have betrayed our trust. Your attitude is unpardonable, irreparable. You must suffer the consequences of your acts. Now you will remain locked in this room until there is a total and profound transformation in your relationship with God and with us, until your regeneration, until your rebirth. Read again your Gospel, the account of Nicodemus and the story of the sinful woman. They both went to Christ seeking to be reborn.

He sets himself to nailing tight the window shutters of the room, one after another. Each nail is driven into her flesh, her freedom, her hopes.

She tries to say something, to defend herself, but the sounds come with difficulty. She trembles in all her being:

—You come to crucify me—to sacrifice me—to damn me.

—I come so you may be reborn to eternal life. Your faith and your salvation are more important than your freedom, or even your life. Your faith and your salvation are more important than all the salvations in the Arab world. No one is going to tear you from our hands. No one will tear you from His hand.

And the blows pound into the wood and into her heart. Papa has cast the stone at her. He wants her death, thinking it is her life. How to explain to him? How to make him understand? How to describe and explain Palestine? How to make the vision of her life alive for him? How to make love triumph without herself also casting the stone? Has Christ not said to turn the other cheek?

Outside, somewhere machine guns are splattering. The entire city seems to be conniving. Doesn't it seek the death of Palestine? Don't they seek her death and the renunciation of her dreams? Her union with P. is condemned and their dream is condemned. It is all Palestine which is imprisoned, nailed down, buried with her. Without and within the blows diminish; the job has been done. Freedoms are controlled, immured, stifled. The caged bird is crushed. Papa looks at her with no remorse. Authority, knowledge, systems and dogmas moving along with him from one blind to the next, from one nail to another, from stone to stone. Papa is satisfied and proud of himself, confident of his Wisdom, confident of his Total Power. Mama has merely to kneel, to accept, to bow down and the little bird has merely to die! All cloistered women, locked up, mutilated, forced to their knees in shame and in despair!

You reap what you sow. *She* broke her promise. A promise is sacred. But that promise was torn out of her by force. All the same, she did make it. It was before, not after, that she should have resisted, said 'no,' stood up for what she believed. It is *before* that Palestine ought to have resisted, said *no* to the intruder, not allowed the invasion. But could she have done so? Had she enough strength for that? Useless to regret, the damage is done. She must go forward. She must be stronger now. She must try to go towards the light. She must learn from the past and move forward. But what can she do now? Isn't it already too late? Has she not closed off her horizon with her own hands? She is shut up in a room, nailed and padlocked. How to see him again? How to speak to him? How to fly with him towards their dream? How to go towards the light and the world of promise and discoveries? How to give to those orphans a belief in the future? How to rebuild upon the strangled bodies, upon the bloodied lips, upon genitals torn out and slashed, upon human segments hacked to pieces and upon an entire city drawn and quartered, ploughed and furrowed with vengeances, hatreds, and injustices?

She feels stifled, as if being asphyxiated breath by breath. How long will she keep hanging on in this tomb? Will her parents dare not to send her to school without a valid excuse for absence, they who vaunt themselves as ones who never tell a lie? The whole city connives with them in everything. It wants the annihilation of her dreams. It wants the death of Palestine. It wants to raze the camps and slaughter the children. It wants to burn whatever seeds of hope planted at Israel's frontier still exist. It wants to crush any union of a Christian young woman and a Muslim man which begins to develop: stifle the chick in its egg. It wants to fix the Cross on all the Palestinian children who stagnate in cold, hunger, misery. It wants to destroy whatever feeds the hope for an Arab world transformed, revolutionized, regenerated.

Outside, shots crack out, bombs explode, flames arise. Somewhere a cry rends the air, fills her soul with fright, penetrates the anguish of her new prison. She is not alone. Someone cries out with her, somewhere. Someone burns in the holocaust so that the flowers of autumn may be reborn, so that the trees may grow again upon the tree-shorn hillocks.

Mama comes in to pray. But all of Mama's sweetness, all her tenderness, all her prayers fail to alter that death which came just now, galvinized by that cry. Mama is bowed down and turned inward by Papa's anger. All women bowed down in the silence of tents and the desert. All women on their knees, enveloped in veils of prayer and abnegation. Life circumcised for eternity. Eyes blinded by tears flowing for eternity. Mama places an icy hand against E.'s forehead. Her forehead burns. She shakes with fever. She falls asleep in the delirium of a mounting fever, unaware of a figure kneeling at the foot of her bed. It is Mama who lifts a prayer to God that somewhere faith may be reborn.

E. dreams that she is on a cliff. Down below, the sea begins to hurl itself in large waves of white foam against the sheer wall. There is a frail little sailboat profiled in the distance, a shadow above which resembles her. She cries out with all her strength. She cries out that she wishes to live, that she wishes to be allowed to live. But the waves strike more and more swiftly. She tries to draw back, but a mass of outstretched hands, black hands and white hands, hands of children and hands of adults, hands of men and hands of women push her, repelling her towards the cliff's edge and toward the waves. The little boat appears to approach her. P. waves vigorously to her with a white kerchief in one hand, in the other he holds the flag of Palestine. And the crowd of hands push at her more and more and with more and more force. She is compelled to leap from the cliff into the flood. But the boat is much too far away. She does not succeed in reaching it. Enormous waves submerge her again and again. She can no longer breathe. She feels herself sinking. Far off, the little boat is also foundering.

She awakes, crying. She hurls herself against the door but it is locked. The scene of the night before flashes upon her: Papa, the nails, the hammer, the blinds, the gun shots, the cry, the death and the dark room. Mama brings food for her to eat, but she refuses. She will make a hunger strike. Her only means of defense. The only way to indicate her existence. To affirm herself, to defend herself, to fight, to take the town by assault, to refuse to die, to cry out against injustices, in spite of the locked door, in spite of Palestine lost forever, in spite of the camp razed, burned, swept away, and all of those deaths which defy counting.

The room appears to shrink, the wardrobes come together. The curtains shudder. One wardrobe tilts dangerously on edge and is going to fall on her, she is certain. The whole room is against her. She fears being encircled and having taken away from her even the power to resist.

And the deserts shall bloom again at His voice. And trees shall put forth new branches. And the Palestinian schools buried beneath the sands shall receive the water of resurrection, which will bring their rebirth, will bring the joy of life to them, will bring them hope. And the children will call out with joy among the palm trees with purple dates shaped like eggs and birds. And waves of sand will be transformed into clear streams of water uncontaminated and pure. And Samir will come to drink the water of his childhood. She will run with him along the roads dusted with pure gold and sunlight. And all the children will follow them with delirious joy of life and of love rediscovered. Promises made will be kept. And the prophecies will come to pass. And she will at last understand the meaning of her anguish.

Bloody-handed, the shutter nails grasped in his hands, Papa looking at her with irony. Jesus crucified for the third time. Jesus refusing the cup and crying out, "Aba, Father." Papa and Mama kneeling on the carpet, praying for her, praying for her salvation, that she accept the narrow and somber way of faith. Words of her Swiss grandmother in her childhood, "Remember all your life what I am going to tell you: 'If there are two roads before you, choose the more difficult one, it is surely the right one, Jesus said: I am the Way the Truth and the Life. No one comes to the Father but by Me. A flower opening must close itself quickly before being too much exposed to rays of danger. It is better to die on this earth in order to be reborn to life eternal, accept always the cross you bear. Take the cross and follow Christ. Always the narrow and somber road of Faith.' "

Mother kneeling at the foot of the bed: woman weighed down, woman humiliated, woman who accepts the Cross to bear all the days of her life. Mary keeping everything in her heart. Mary kneeling before her Son with the animals in the manger. The gentleness of Mary ready ever for sacrifice for Father and Son. All the women shut up in the stable, and mutilated sewn up and violated. All women accepting the Cross, the sword which spays them, thanking God for his gift of Grace.

And Papa leaning over her, waving the flag of Truth in one hand, nails and hammer in the other, telling her to pray to the other Father, to give her life into His hands, so that He may lead her to the longed for harbor. Papa overwhelmed by his Wisdom and Omnipotence and overwhelming her like a fly caught in a web. Papa speaking to her of love and humility, of obedience and submission. Papa with eyes filled with tears. Papa weeping for her. Tears falling upon her. Sincerity of Papa who puts forth his dogma and his system. Papa who feels guided by the Father on High to set himself up as a prophet to see what others do not see, but not to see what others see. Papa intransigent with all he sees.

But she cries out, she cries out that she does not want his dogma. That she wishes to live, that she wishes to know and to understand herself, to understand life and that enormous thirst for justice which she feels in the depths of her being. That she wants no more nails, she wants no more blood, she wants to take Jesus from the Cross in order to search into her very depths once and for all, to find in what ways she resembles Jesus and will be able to live in Jesus, far from the dogmas and systems erected by all the Papas of this world. She refuses to die now. She refuses their vison of the world. She screams, she screams, she screams.

And and echo of her screams rings through the city. Hundreds of voices cry along with her in the city. The women imprisoned in the city cry with her. Women rebel along with her and break their chains along with her. And the Palestinian children in their camps clap their hands with joy and exuberance. And the whole city resounds with the echoes of her screams.

Slowly, she returns from her long journey of fever, of delirium, and of prayers lifted at the foot of the bed by Papa and Mama. She tries to rise but she can hardly stand on her own feet. The mirror gives back to her an image of herself which she does not recognize: face small and thin, two hollow circles of purple and black beneath her eyes. She looks at her hands. They are quite thin and discolored, spotted with dark shadows. The nails, the blood. Papa, the hammer, the entreaties of

34

Papa, her cry: "Aba, Papa, I want nothing from that cup. I wish to live." Hunger strike and resistance, and at last the Resistance and the battle in the camps. A refusal to let the world come to a halt. A refusal to let oneself be crushed upon an earth which already stinks of putrefaction. An immense faith in letting speak the blood of life which flows within her. Then, the illness. She has been unable to make a long resistance. The illness came to sweep away her strength, to drain off her courage, to sap her veins of the red blood which had enflamed them with new strength. Will she have the strength to rejoin him, to set out for those horizons which he had described to her, towards that desert city where the children await them, perched in trees, eager to follow, waiting to fly off with them and find marvelous dates and fruits of life?

Papa and Mama approach her and look at her with anxiety. Papa carries a large package wrapped in newspaper. It is smoked herring. That will excite an appetite. That will cure fever and worries. It is the food of pardon and recuperation. It is the manna of reconciliation. Papa is preparing it for her, so that she will return to life and to the faith of her childhood. Papa sprinkles it with olive oil and lemon—the unction of eucharistic bread: the taking in through the pores of the sweet and vitalizing liquid. Papa feeds her fat mouthfuls in magnetic silence. Mama breaks the bread and watches her with solicitude. The bread passes from hand to hand, confirming the desire to understand, to share, to rediscover family bonds. Papa pulls out the nails, opens the windows. Sunlight rushes in like a sea. It enters blatantly, penetrating the shadows of the room, piercing into her inert, anemic limbs. E. is dazzled and falls back upon the bed, seeing Papa and Mama as if through a fog, her feelings anxious and her glance filled with anguish. Is she going to die?

Mama speaks of Switzerland where they will be going in a few days. They will put her in a Bible Camp with her sister. She will be up in the mountains and near to God. She will get well and will find peace again, and life in Jesus Christ, salvation and pardon. She will breathe the pure air of the eternal mountain peaks and she will understand the beauty and the grandeur of the Almighty, of the One who had chosen them according to His plan. She will see the beauty of the Eternal. And in her heart something of that which they had sown there in her childhood will be reborn, will flower again and conduct her toward the desired haven. There she will know that they were right, that she ought never to have rebelled, that she should have accepted everything as her brothers and her sister did. And, just like those who reason with some bit of intelligence, accept that one must yield oneself before Papa, that one must accept the family and the institutions created by God, for these are a dike against the evil and the sin which spread more and more throughout the world.

E. tries to see P. before her departure to Switzerland. The city is dangerous. Armored trucks filled with soldiers in strange uniforms pass endlessly through streets leading to the south. A new summer is announcing itself, a summer more cruel and more frightening than all the others. Already the heat has come in with a fury. Already the planes from the south have bombed schools, burned children, sown panic, heated people's tempers. Already the population has settled itself into its differences, its recriminations, its diversions, its hates and its desire for vengeance.

Yes, she feels something has died in her and something else is being born in her. And she has not yet come to a definition of just what it is. Like Samir, she buried herself in that cave where she has lived for several days. Like Samir, she wishes to rediscover the magic box of her childhood. She feels waves rise in her, higher and swifter; they are a tide which will swallow her to transform her, leaving the shore intact in spite of all, a shore of fine sand, burning with glossy and eternal pebbles. The waves are always new but they are part of the same sea. It is a love which she feels being born in her, love which always permits rebirth and new beginnings in spite of everything.

She succeeds in meeting him in a little side street near the school. It is very dangerous to see him again after all that has happened: a Muslim man and a Christian young woman loving each other under a sky of hatred, in a country divided by dogmas and religions. They risk death, assassination, there in the open road under that sun which crushes and kills.

In a few words she explains the situation to him. It is necessary that upon her return from Switzerland he have everything prepared for their departure. Right after her return it will be necessary to flee, it will be necessary that together they quit this city which seeks to slay them, the institutions and dogmas which encircle them, more and more tightly to stifle and demolish them. She is afraid of reliving what she has just lived through. She is afraid of dying a second time, and this time forever. The crucifixion can occur only once. The other occurrences are but mirages. And nothing good can come out of something false, inauthentic, created from an illusion, a pretension, a superficiality, a facade. She is fearful of experiencing again the dark room, the cries in the night from beyond the blinds nailed shut, the cries of women of her country from the other side of a wall she cannot scale. And that impression of being asphyxiated, of sinking more and more quickly into fever and delirium.

P. reassures her. Everything is already prepared. He will wait for her. And at the end of the summer they will cross together that sea which she is going to cross a few days hence. Together they will go to that region of sands and promises where they will work to make justice rule at last for his people. She must restore herself, must find strength for the task which awaits her. They shall at last win out together over the differences which separate them, for they love one another.

He looks upon her tenderly. For a second, they press together in the euphoria of their promise. A dangerous fraction of a second in an atmosphere which forbids male and female to touch, no matter what their religious denomination. They separate, revived by that embrace signifying promises made in spite of fears and prohibitions, in spite of the heavens black with smoke and ashes, and in spite of the long summer before them which will separate them and which is preparing for the horror of new carnages and new atrocities.

Slowly the ship leaves the dock. A humid breeze is blowing. E. leans, elbows on handrail, gazing at the Lebanese mountains shining in the distance. What a beautiful land so ravaged by war. What name to give such hatred? What face to put upon the carnage? What bodies to recognize among the corpses? How could the natural hospitality and generosity of its citizens give birth to such monstrosities?

The night is electric and the waves seem to flash back an oily gold. The sound of the ship's moving through the waves awakens in her a feeling of vitality which she thought she had lost. Perhaps peace will come after all. Perhaps the fires on the mountains will turn into torchlights. Perhaps the canons will turn into flowers and birds. And perhaps the vines and the olive trees will pour out their wine and their oil to citizens eager to pardon, to forget, and to be reconciled with one another.

She thinks of the end of summer when she will look upon that same sea, that same shore, those same mountains, united with him, going toward the same goal, bent upon its endless bounty. Will there then be more of peace and hope in these mountains which now do nothing but rearm? Will someone or something succeed in piercing the masks of horror and bitterness which hide the true faces of the people of her country? Once again she is seized by the feeling that she must begin with herself, so that that understanding may help her to understand others, to reach a solution. It is painful but essential to make her past revive, to recall that past and to learn from that past in order to move forward towards the light.

She loves these boat trips. They give her an illusion of freedom. The ship cutting through the water. Her hair free in the breeze. And all the people with whom she can speak and engage in conversations about their lives, which so little resemble her own. It is funny how everyone seems to speak of the same things: the latest film, the newest style, the latest recording, latest song. Where is the war which has destroyed their lives up to the moment of boarding ship? They seem to have forgotten it, or perhaps never did experience it. Well hidden in their panelled and protected villas often situated on mountain heights inaccessible to combatants, they have looked upon the carnage from afar, going to some local club or cinema to forget their remorse.

At Alexandria, new passengers come on board. She notices a young Egyptian woman with a sad expression and nervous gestures, smoking cigarette after cigarette. E. is at once attracted by her independent demeanor, her mannerisms of an emancipated woman, mixed with a serious, calm, and soft expression, a combination which one rarely finds among Arab women.

The young woman seems fearful. Often she looks behind her furtively, with apprehension, as though she is being followed. She is like a hunted bird trying to fly off. She slips behind lifeboats, hides in out-of-the-way corners of the ship, losing her concentration to the sea in contemplation which seems painful. How to meet this woman, this Egyptian? How to get into a conversation with her?

One day, the Egyptian, who has noticed her also, offers her a cigarette. But E. doesn't dare smoke it. If Papa and Mama should see her! But she holds it a long while between her fingers. It is a way to establish contact. There is a whole new world almost within her grasp. A forbidden garden of tempting and juicy fruits, with a smooth and pungent pulp. It is the entrance into a world which will thrill her, open a road to knowledge and wisdom, into which she will hurl herself breathlessly, trying to make up for lost time, trying to discover the reason for the emotions she has been unable to control.

E. dares to light up. Her first cigarette. She breathes in the bitter and strong odor which gives her a feeling of euphoria which she will often thereafter try again to find. The ship cutting the water, her hair to the wind, the first cigarette, the sea air—a combination of freedom and exhaltation which draws her closer to the Egyptian.

The Egyptian asks questions: where does E. come from? Where is E. going? Why is she so nervous when she smokes? Is she being watched? And while speaking, the Egyptian looks behind herself as if she also is being watched; she has a nervous tic which makes her eyes blink and gives her aspect a feverish intensity. She looks out across the sea as if to an infinite horizon.

E. does not know why, but she opens herself up to the Egyptian. She tells her of her life and her plans. She tells her of the war, of steel and death. She tells of camps of starvation and misery. She tells of the city stitched through with hatreds and vengeances. She tells of her own family and their beliefs, of their faith in a transcendent salvation and of the evangelical tent where every evening a crowd rushes together to forget its problems. E. makes the Egyptian party to her doubts and fears, and to her discovery of love. E. speaks of P., of their plans, of the desert country to which they shall journey at the end of the summer to realize their dream—of love, of peace, and of hope.

But the woman begins to cry, at first softly, then harder and harder. Now her body shakes, shudders, and she sobs. E. tries vainly to calm her. E. strokes her hair tenderly. E. questions: what has she said so frightening and anguishing? Is it the description of the war and the camps which so bothers her?

The Egyptian turns towards E. a hunted look, a face wet with bitter tears. E. is seized with fright and helplessness in the presence of this distress bursting forth, this wound beginning to open, this show of bitterness, this pervasive pain. The Egyptian wipes away her tears and stiffens herself. She looks at E. with intensity and in a voice hoarse and still trembling, cries out at her:

—Do not go with that man. Never go to that country where you think you are going to realize some dreams, where you think you can live and be free, where you think a woman is respected and can stand side by side with a man and go forward with equality and mutual respect. I, I am coming from there! I am fleeing from it. I hide because I am in fear of being pursued. I am afraid that one of my brothers may have boarded this ship and will take me back by force or kill me and toss my body into the sea. It would be easy, who would know? Besides, who would punish him, since Society approves of such crimes and even encourages them?

The Egyptian tosses her cigarette butt into the sea, sadly watching it disappear, snatched up by the waves. An omen? A mirror? A reflection? The echo of one soul in search of another soul, in search of communication, of understanding, of flight over the walls, partitions, veils. She lights another cigarette angrily. Her eyes are fixed upon the horizon, her brow furrowed, her neck extended. Her mouth shows again a bitter grimace and her hands tremble. She turns again toward E., seems to hesitate to tell her something. She stares at E. a long while. Then she speaks out all at once, as though to free herself of a burden which she has been carrying since she boarded the ship.

—Do you know what they do to their women over there, at the age of puberty—or even before, or before marriage if inadvertently a woman has succeeded in avoiding the surveillance of the elder women? Do you know the suffering of the flesh itself, the burning, the rending, the tearing out of that delicate and sensitive organ lodged between the two legs—the excision, the ablation of the organ called the clitoris, an erotic nipple, and the minor labia and the major labia also cut, mutilated, excised, and the wounds which bleed and bleed and bleed neverendingly, and the days and weeks of immobility in the dark, legs fastened by cords, the body shaken with spasms, and the feeling of shame, terrible shame, and the cries of women, and the piercing grief which never ends when you know that your body will never again be as it was, when you recognize that something which would give you the power to vibrate, to feel, has been stolen from you, when you are afraid of hemorrhaging, when you know that your body has been transgressed, that you have already been violated, that a part of your life has been taken away and that instead you have been sewn up, tied, closed so that you may never again breathe or open yourself to life, to tenderness, to the freshness of a desert morning? And the old women cackle, cackle, cackle, happy to revenge themselves for what life has taken away from them, from them too; happy to see that the flow of blood continues, that the suffering is not stopped at their own bodies, that the infernal circle perpetuates itself and turns and turns and turns. What are you doing? You? Why don't you break that circle as I am doing? Why not rebel before it is too late, before you also become an *excisée*? You have lived in war. You have seen the horror of blood spilled in the streets, on the earth, external to yourself, but if you were to encounter the blood and the shame and the horrors which you have told me about, the mutilated bodies, the sex organs ripped away, the corpses violated, if you should encounter all that internally in your very own flesh, then what would you do?

E. has the impression of talking to a madwoman. She does not understand very well the thrust of the Egyptian's words. Sexuality has always been a taboo subject at home and the young woman's descriptions give her a feeling which she cannot fully identify. She feels a sharp revulsion at new kinds of violence more cruel than those she has already known. Her sensibility has been exacerbated, and contradictory feelings are insinuated by the woman's descriptions. The Egyptian's expression has taken on a sinister color. Her face is pale as death. All her movements appear concentrated in the cigarette whose red tip burns with ash glowing purple and violet. Her body begins a nervous and spasmodic trembling which she can't manage to control. She looks in every direction with fright. One might say a little bird caught in a great net. Her large eyes, dark and sad, fix upon E. again for a long spell with the wild and ravaged expression of a being who no longer knows where to go nor to whom to turn. Then she disappears behind a lifeboat like a child who has just been stopped for something unjust, monstrous, devastating, and who does not wish to show her tears, who does not wish to let herself give way to her affliction before another person or even a mirror.

During the following days, E. searches vainly for the Egyptian, who seems to have disappeared. E. walks the ship's deck, looks behind the lifeboats, but there is no trace of the woman. Had she really existed? Did E. not dream the entire scene? Then she remembers certain words of the Egyptian. "Perhaps one of my brothers is following me." What if that were so? It is the kind of thing which occurs every day in that country of hers. Save the family's honor at any cost. Cleanse the honor in blood or in the sea. E. leans forward to contemplate the sea which suddenly appears dark and menacing. A terrible feeling of anguish clutches at her throat. She would like to know. She would like to find out. She looks into cabins through their portholes; she lifts the canvas which covers vehicles and crates, follows the paths through coils of cordage. And always she turns back to to the sea which appears impassive and cruel. Why can't it cast up all its secrets just for once? Why this calm when every day it swallows up bodies and corpses and feeds itself on secrets like the Sphinx which devours whoever does not understand what it wants him to understand? Suddenly she fears that she is beginning to contemplate her own image which flickers in the waves raised by the force of the wind.

> For behold! the day comes
> Ardent as a furnace
> All the proud and all the wicked will be like stubble.
> The day which comes will enfold them
> Says the Eternal of the Armies
> It will leave them neither root nor branch.
> But for you who fear My Name there will arise
> The sunshine of justice
> And your healing will be under its wings
> You will go forth and leap like calves of the manger
> It will return the hearts of the fathers to their children
> And the hearts of children to their fathers
> Ere I should come to destroy the cursed land.

E. has gone back to a Bible Camp where Mama and Papa wish her to restore herself, to immerse herself in the primal waters from the springs of her childhood, that she be rebaptized, purified, transformed to a new life, that in regarding the sublime mountains of eternal snow she recognize the grandeur of the All-Powerful, that she kneel before the Eternal Father and thank Him for having led her to the longed-for haven of His Name. Each evening the master of the camp gathers all around for a Bible study and for prayers which are raised in great simplicity in the calm freshness of nights overwhelmed by the sublime Alps.

41

How far away is Beruit, barricaded with engines of death; how far away the olive trees, the orange trees, and the apple trees frightfully twisted, the vine clinging desperately to ruins of a wall and the mornings red with the blood of nights!

One day she takes a side path to be alone, to reflect, to think about that past, stormy with war and violence, which she has left behind, far away at the other shore of the sea, and to consider that future which awaits her in the desert, which throbs under the sunlight golden and vital. She is well into the forest when suddenly the name of Papa, pronounced distinctly a couple of paces away, makes her shudder and stop short. It is Mister A. and Madam M. of the Bible group, seated on a bench behind the tree which hides her. She holds her breath, struck by bits of phrases which she begins to grasp and which more and more quickly, and more and more strongly, strike at her heart and paralyzed her with horror and fright!

—These Arabs . . . there's nothing to be done with them . . . they are liars of the worst kind. It is impossible to confide in them or to believe what they say . . . their words are always broken . . . their oaths are always false, two-faced. You've been there. How one has to bargain for everything! They never say what they really think.

—Yes, they have, it appears, a whole series of fabricated polite phrases which they repeat on different occasions without attributing to them any true and profound meaning. That's certainly an aberrant mentality. It's no wonder God had to set apart a Chosen People under such circumstances, since they were surrounded by so much falseness and hypocrisy.

—Yes, God is just and Israel will win out in spite of its weakness and frailty. Just as David triumphed over the giant Goliath, Israel will bring Victory over Evil. It is the miracle of the desert which blooms again, of the fig tree which burgeons, and of the vine which greens. Israel, she is the miracle of the Resurrection.

E. sees heads which she recognizes. Two persons of the most fervent ones in the group who are ever praying with warmth and zeal, who are ever the first to rise to show proof of faith, who are always quick to give instructions to the young people.

She hides behind some bushes, devastated by this revelation, her breath stopped by the enormity of their own hypocrisy.

The blows rain upon her from all directions. How long the road will be! Swiss and Arab: an unpardonable mixture, a mixture making the child cry before its birth, a mixture which recrucifies the dead. The West regarding the East with all its arrogance, superiority, and affluence, striking and crushing the East. The West abandoning the East after gorging itself, eating all its butter and all its olives and all its

42

fruits, and after killing all its birds. The West enriched by the sweat of the Black, the sinews of the Black, the bent back of the Black, its machines oiled by the olive trees of the *fellah*, its blood renewed by the vine of the *bougnoute* and all its towns built upon the heavy groaning of slaves.

Man has reduced God and made Him in his image. A twisted image, tortuous as he is himself, imperfect man, hypocrite and liar. All-just God who judges from above. And man does not see that in place of letting God speak in him, it is he who speaks and creates God and creates his God and writes His laws which circumscribe, subjugating man and cutting God down.

But no, God truly is not like that stunted image. God comes to free, to love, to understand, to give joy and hope. But no, faith is not a sword which judges and severs the black from the white, the good from the evil, or lines men up against a wall to measure who is the tallest, who is most upright.

Faith is a flame which grows with love and with a desire to understand; with prayers in one's room, alone face to face with God. Faith is shown to those who accept it and open themselves to it, and faith engenders in them a flood of love, of tenderness, of understanding. It is a long process of growing.

Don't hurl at our heads your God whom you have shrouded with your dogmas, your Sunday morality, a God tarnished by your rotted institutions, by your churches which go through rituals memorized and not felt.

To those who speak to God everyday, He reveals His face, simple and pure. He teaches them how to love the men who do them evil, how to walk upright and not judge all those around them who stumble as they walk. He gives them strength to understand what will bring peace to the world. He gives this peace to those who let God speak in them and who will extend a hand to the dispossessed and those who suffer.

Faith, for those who agree to grow with it, is a liberation, a flame of love, of generosity, and goodness. It is an increasing of spirit by the breath of life and peace which turns away from one self and towards the other. Faith is love, not judgment.

Men and Women of the Third World,
Raise your voices, made hoarse by centuries of slavery
Hold out your hands, and your arms broken by chains.
And your backs bruised by whips,
Straighten them.

The glance of the veiled woman shows strange lights which speak a new language
The painful arms of the black man have a power which rends the curtains of brass
The woman attacked has a soft response which cauterizes hate and vengence.
The woman mutilated has taken the clotted blood on her wounds and made from it flowers of love and gardens of tenderness.

And instead of striking where one has been struck, one takes the flower of clotted blood to make a shield from it; one opens roads and one travels the rivers which lead to a world which once brandished all its swords and all its canons and all its guns—a world which, in the face of this new opening, falls to the ground grovelling in its downfall, all aggression extinguished by the sudden revelation of the dazzling light of passion and hope.

And the small child again finds the way of the river
And the men and women march together, side by side,
toward the light.

The ship slowly departs the Lebanese shore. They are side by side: a Muslim man and a Christian woman, an impossible mixture, but realized, thanks to love and thanks to faith and thanks to the belief in a better world, to a common goal of the triumph of the forces of life and tenderness. The ship parts the waves, the same sea which she crossed several months ago with her family. Today she is with *him*. She studies his proud profile. She loves his expression, thirsting for the dream. His caressing hands take hers and draw her toward the cabin-bunk.

It seemed only yesterday that she had entered a similar cabin where the Egyptian had shown her the scar between her thighs, the monstrous blue cicatrix, the erotic nipple torn out; old women cackling, blood flowing to the earth, a cross to bear, a crescent to brandish, infinite suffering inflicted by force and without respite, the halting of joy, pleasure amputated, ecstacy asphyxiated, womanhood demolished.

> Women crying in every tent
> Women forming a frenzied group
> Screaming their grief, their desire to live
> Tears flowing even to the sea
> Tears merging with the foam
> Scars of tissue blue and violet, buried in the flood,
> And the little girl begging her mother to hold her warm within the walls, to save her from the knife and the blood—
> And the little girl moving toward the sea, into the sea.

> Marry as it please you, man,
> Two three four wives—
> But if you fear it isn't fair,
> Take a single wife
> Or else your captives in a war,
> That are worth more to you
> Than to be unable to sustain
> The needs of a large family.

Today he has encircled her with his robust arms. He carries her to the cabin bunk, humid, sea-salty. He caresses her with passion. Her whole being vibrates next to that man whom she followed because she believes in him, because he stands as a symbol of liberty and truth, because a hand has brought them together despite the forces of destruction which surround them and in spite of the violence of a war which has planted dehumanized corpses in a soil plowed with vengeances.

His arms strain more strongly. Her trembling increases.

> The end of the myth
> Woman feeble, man strong,
> Woman earth, man plow
> Myth fixed, rooted
> Weakness, aching
> Grief
> Sea of endless woe.

He plows her. She yields. She lets go of herself like a being totally devoid of vision, like a non-being. She gives in once more to fate. May he guide me, He. It is he who has the vision. It is he who will show me the way: I am the Way, the Truth, and the Life. None come to the Father but by Me. This is, by all rights, My way; therefore follow it! Do not walk those roads which would distance you from the Way of God. Behold, that is what he orders you. Perhaps you will fear him! Palestine, Christ, the man of Jaffa, the Way which plows her, the sword which quarters her, the nails which crucify her. My God, grant that this cup not be too bitter!

Penetrate me, oh penetrate me and may the torture end so that you may be satiated, satisfied, so that all your desires may be fulfilled, so that, at last, you walk down your road to Damascus. May you lead me beside the still waters, where you and I may live in peace in the green pastures, where we may again find Palestine, where you and I together may rebuild Palestine, thanks to you because you have penetrated me, because you have taken me, because I have yielded myself, because all has its end in your vision of the world, in that emblem which you wear about your neck, emblem of Palestine, symbol of the resurrection and the life, symbol of a new world, of new values, transformed into seeds which fall, which rain upon the word carrying the rebirth so long awaited.

I am there in your arms and you do not even see me. You see nothing of me but a morsel of flesh which you hold in your arms, that mythical being which you turn into putty to mold, which you mold according to an idea preconceived, taught for centuries, learned from childhood when you were only a small boy in the great house of Jaffa, where your father used to say to you, "You see, my son, a plow and oxen are needed to plow a field and seeds are needed to inseminate it. Thereafter, you must pray God that He cause his mercy to rain down from heaven." And you, you listened to him, believing that you would always have a land, a plow and oxen and believing that God would smile always from heaven, sending you rain and blessing, filling you with, manna.

You are expert, my friend. Your fingers penetrate me enough to make me feel that there is something extra that exists in you and which might be born of you and me, a spark of understanding, a world of tenderness if only you would allow yourself to listen to your inner self, to let speak that which is deep within you and which you hide beneath the agility of your fingers stroking over me. And you enter my flesh expertly knowing your way. You know the convolutions of my mythology, but you do not see me. You cannot see me because you will not look at me. You are too wrapped up in viewing yourself. And I, I remain here, my hands empty, my womb empty, my thighs parted, all my being thirsty for tenderness, for encounter, for discovery, all my being awaiting that the explosion come to an end and that my flowering may begin—so that I may talk about my hopes and that your eyes will look at and see me.

Woman who races towards the light
Woman whose joy is cut down
Torn away at its root
Woman who works with patience at the heart of her being
So that other women may see life
Woman frozen in her silence
Woman crucified in her pain
And the little child leaves the maternal breast
And it launches out toward the river where the dragon awaits it
The monster with seven heads which prepares the ending.

The shore line is profiled in the distance. It is a line, flat and yellow, a yellow of gold. It is the desert which enters the sea. E. is gliding toward her future. A silence has settled between them. It is not a mutual silence. It is not a silence of understanding and meaning. It is a wall of silence. It is a silence which separates them, which parts them, which sows doubts in her. What has become of the moments shared in face of that same sea when a vision of the future hurled her toward him, when their two beings were united in a common goal?

E. studies him. His profile is hard. His eyes lose themselves in the distance. She takes his hand and tries to interlace his fingers with hers, to try to warm herself in his flowing life, in his vitality, in the blood which flows in his fingers, in his odor, in his fire, to try to overcome that fear she feels surging in her.

—You must veil yourself when we arrive at the village. A woman must be veiled if she wishes to be respected. There's no reason for you to be any different from the other women. I shall be called upon because of my role as a teacher to take on great responsibilities with respect to the authorities of the neighboring city. I would not wish to have people talk. Even now, bringing a Christian woman with me will cause a scandal.

E. remains silent. She ought to speak, but she remains silent. What could she say to him? Yet she ought to speak. And the scenes of her childhood begin again—when she tried to confront her father. It was then, when she was a child, that she should have won the battle. She ought to have faced her father down, not let herself be nailed into her room. Die rather than be crucified. What, what could she have done and what can she do now? She doesn't wish to die, not now, not yet. . . .

    Woman on her knees, hands crossed
    Hands extended toward the world
    Locked up in her indifference and her torpor
    Woman bent double
    Broken, crushed by her brother's chains
    Woman bearing the pains of the world

    O, P. . . . all the P.'s
    A very furnace which burns with hatred
    A very fire which consumes with force
    Fire which obliterates woman
    Which nails her, which stops her speech
    Which renders her to ashes.

    And the woman takes the cinders and of them makes flowers
    She weaves a curtain of threads of love and tenderness
    Which she places between her and man

So that he may learn to do otherwise.
She takes the child which she hides in her bosom
Far from the face of the Serpent
She distances the toothless mouth of the Serpent from the
head of the child
And she breathes life into the child's heart
That he may become a new man
And there, where hatred has struck
She plants, she plants and she waters
She waters with her tears the new tree.

Refuse to wear the veil? And why? E. wants to penentrate that world of the veil, world of women behind the veil, world of beings in silence, world of waiting, world of words never spoken, world of glances which question, world of mouths sealed shut, of child after child, world of gestures which cross each other without meaning; that dark world, world of despair and suffering, world which calls her to it because she has been chosen to understand it.

She draws back her hand which has become icy. Her heart beats so hard that she fears it will burst. The ship is already quite close to the dock. Heat rising from the land envelops them. It is a humid heat which sticks to the skin. A crowd is pressing toward the exit. For an instant, she is seized with panic. Wouldn't be better now to hurl herself into the water, to annihilate herself once and for all, never to have to confront that life which awaits her out there—in the stifling heat of days which will never be clear and fresh, with that man who has become a total stranger to her and who represents a world of women which she is going to discover. She must win victory for them. Or, at least, one among them must win out.

P.'s brother is already there awaiting them. He wears the same somewhat mocking smile she had noticed on P. in the beginning, when he had been waiting for her outside the gate at school. The brother is staring fixedly at her. E. puts her hands to her face. All this will be different when heavy cloth makes separation between her face and his seeing. She, she will see him as she sees him now, but he will see of her only a shining fabric which hides the features of the one who looks at him. He will sense that she is looking at him, but that is all. There will be no communication.

—The whole village is expecting you, the brother says, I have brought clothing more suitable for your new functions.

How he says that! What irony is in his voice! How he stares at her! As if he would rape her. Does P. notice? He is too busy getting the clothes out of the valise which are going to transform them, disguise

49

them as new man and woman, called upon to play a new role in an old country with ancestral customs. He hands her a long bulky cloth, a sort of cape to envelop and hide, and a black mask, bluish-violet. The mask is divided into halves between the forehead and the chin by a transverse bar which gives the effect of a second nose. On each side there is a slit for the eyes: peep-holes. The mask is held in place by four silvered elastics, attached two above and two below the ears, all tied at the back of the head. There is also a little transparent black veil spangled with silver and gold.

—This is the sign that you are a young bride and that your husband is not a poor man, says the brother waving the light veil.

It is very hot and E. wonders if she will be able to endure all those heavy and black envelopes. But already the two brothers are hurrying her: first the mask, then the little veil, then the large veil. The cloth and the elastics squeeze her head and she feels a migraine rising, her temples throbbing. The slits for the eyes are little more than pinholes and her vision is framed in darkness. She fears that she will suffocate, and die of asphyxiation. Her arms alone, unclad and free, reach toward the opening and to the heavens in a gesture of supplication and revolt. She looks to the brother, but he is no longer looking at her.

> The woman shoved behind the veil
> Is forced inwardly upon herself.
> She beats against the walls of her heart
> And her blows rebound against the veil
> She regards from the interior of the veil
> Her past, her present, and her future
> Which are but one some image
> She cannot even cry
> For tears invisible
> Mark only the skin
> Behind the veil.
> What others see is never a true reflection.

The carriage rolls along a dusty road. It is the desert sand which stretches to infinity. She is shrouded in her veil and she is silent, her face turned against the window towards the countryside which comes to her through the carriage, through the veil. She no longer belongs to the world of people. All at once she has crossed behind the veil, she has passed beyond the inner walls, she has entered into a world of silence, a world of mystery. Breathing is difficult. Will she be able to endure this world of abnegation? She has been crushed. From infancy, she has been suppressed, stifled. However, she has already struck back, she has already cried out, she has already broken, shaken off the yoke of Papa. But for this one, will she have enough strength?

Up ahead, the two men are talking. She no longer can understand what they are saying. Already the segregation has been established, their words carry no meaning for her. The language has become a vehicle, like the carriage itself, an established instrument, an instrument of power, a machine to make money, violins which speak in discord. And they talk, they talk. They talk business, they talk money, they talk authority.

There in the back, she is no longer anything: an object which has been cast aside, a black hulk which one leads about, which one must take to the house, which one must penetrate through most easy orifices so that the hulk will produce little ones, many little ones, from the hulk and P., between their dreams and . . .

The serpent hisses
The woman scratches the wall with her nails, with her hands
She strikes and strikes
Only an echo replies
She wishes to see the sea, she wishes to find an outlet
The serpent is very near the child's head
The child cries and the woman lifts it up
And hides it under the veil and her torn clothes
Her hands and her nails are bloody, her feet bruised,
The serpent hisses along the wall
And the woman is afraid.

The carriage penetrates into the village. A crowd of neighbors, friends, relatives and children are waiting for them in the enclosure of their new dwelling. The enclosure is in the form of a rectangular court, surrounded by low-roofed houses. The houses abut one another: houses locked, courtyard surrounded by walls, walls enclosed by other walls. There are many children who stare at them, out of round open eyes. Their staring strikes at her heart. They are the same stares which had invaded her when she visited the Palestinian camp: inquiring looks, the new looks of childhood, gleams of hope, looks which seek to understand, looks which pierce one through.

But for them what possibly can she represent? The black hulk moving in, the new arrival, the Christian, the foreigner? Where are the dreams she and P. had before the infinite sea and sky, when he had held her hand, caressing it, and talking to her of all those for whom they would build a new world? What message can she now take to them, a woman transformed in shape, a woman locked up, a woman enveloped, a woman wrapped up, sewed up, restricted by the veil?

She looks at all the children and extends her hands towards them, a gesture of despair, of anguish, of a desire to reach out, to understand and to alter, of a desire to branch out, to bud, to blossom. But no one sees her gesture and no one knows her anguish.

She enters one of the rooms which will be her home. She must leave her shoes outside. It is a large room, rectangular with carpets of lively colors on the floor. All around it there is a raised bench for sitting, fitted with embroidered pillows. Behind it, on the wall, hangs a cloth with geometric designs in striking colors. At the far end of the room is the bed, covered with an eiderdown, egg-plant purple. Across from the bed is an armoire decorated all over with delicate Islamic motifs in soft blue, mauve and rose. The room is quite bright and pleasant. On the floor, there is a large tray covered by a straw bonnet. She seats herself on the floor and notices that it is not very clean. There are grease spots and crumbs everywhere. A woman lifts the bonnet and offers her fruit: mandarins, bananas, apples. A crowd of flies swarms above them.

All about her, the women busy themselves preparing coffee and pastries. Odors of orange blossom, saffron, ginger spread in the enclosure. She looks at the women who look at her, looks exchanged behind the veil. They are all behind large veils and they look at each other with connivance and a mixture of affection and understanding. Their looks are enheartening. Not since she quit the family home has she had this feeling of well-being. Just like Mama's prayer, the spontaneous goodness and generosity which are born of suffering and oppression, of a belief that it serves better to close ranks and try to live in harmony, faced by this man's world, by segregation, by the veil.

Desert night has fallen, night heavily charged with stars, night of the veil and of silence. The women have gone back into their houses and the children are asleep. She is waiting apprehensively. What will this night bring? Will he be able to get beyond the different layers of the veils which separate them? Will he be able to get her to speak and himself to speak? Will they be able to establish contact with each other?

E. waits in silence, a silence opaque and troubling, an eternity of silence. Why does the woman always wait? Why this abnegation? Why this passivity? Why this servility? Could any truth come out of such a meeting? Her hands are moist. She dampens them with orange-blossom water, softness of flowers, feeling of perfume. It is so fresh and good. She removes her veil, her mask. She undresses in order to bathe herself in that freshness and softness which bring back a feeling of life, which calm the nerves now strained and taut.

She moistens her breasts, her vagina, her abdomen, and the nape of her neck with orange-blossom water. She rubs herself with oil of amber and musk and slowly caresses herself, seeking out and identifying each part of her body. Will she be able to communicate to him these contours, these hollows, these curves, this form—her body? Will he speak to her of his own?

He has come in and he stares at her astonished. His eyes light up with desire at the sight of her nude body, glowing in the moonlight. He presses her mouth passionately.

—How beautiful you are! I want children from you.

He paws her, he grabs her, he penetrates her. He wants children from her. He expects her womb to produce the knowledge which he refuses to her. He wants her to open herself to give and not to take, so as to produce, to serve, to be useful. He wants her womb to not be sterile, to not be cursed by dryness, by the desert wind which burns everything. He wants to prove to his whole entourage that he knows how to sow seed, that the grain is good, and that Allah blesses the harvest.

E. arches her body against the assault. She has to struggle. She must make him understand that there is more in her than children, that there is a creative force which is trying to escape, that there is a whole language which she would love to sketch to him, to weave for him, to shape for him, so that together they might take up the threads one by one and build the world they had so desired, that she thought they had wished for together.

She arches her body against his. She digs her fingers into his flesh, but P. feels nothing. These acts excite him and delight him. He is intense in his pleasure. He watches himself play. She is the mirror in which he sees himself. His whole body relaxes against her palms, against her pressure, against all communication. He falls asleep in the folds of her veils.

Nights follow days and each night it all begins again: her hopes, her anguish, her desires bullied, blocked unappreciated. Each night her viscera are tortured and drained. Each night she arches herself against a man who has already installed himself in his sheathe, a man sure of himself and his place in society, a man who will have his way and who can have any woman he wants. He needs only lift his little finger to have women at his feet, to make slaves of them, round bodies which will docilely wait for him at night, women who will open to let him pleasure himself, to let him relax his nerves strained by a day's work in the city.

She is not a fool. She knows that his law permits him to take other women. All the women who surround her share a man. They don't complain. They are fixed in submission and the expectation of death. From time to time the birth of a child reminds them that their fate is not wholly useless, reminds them that through them life goes onward, that they perpetuate the cycles of generations.

The women begin whispering among themselves as they look upon E.'s abdomen. It is always quite flat in spite of the belabored nights, and P. is bothered. He wants children, many children. A flat abdomen—it is a bad sign. It means that his semen has not taken hold and he has wasted his efforts. It is perhaps a sign that the die has been cast and thus his desires will never be fulfilled.

Each night he doubles his efforts and E. wishes for a child. She dreams of it. Often, at night, she wakes up, hands moist and heart pounding, believing that she has held in her arms the soft body of a silky-haired baby which sucks at her breast. It has become an intense need, this wish for a child, a physical desire, a desire which comes from her very depths, and comes from her past of oppression and her present closed in on every side. This present time, which ought to have realized her most precious dreams! "I want a child. Perhaps he—perhaps *she*—will come to realize those things I wished to accomplish, the great work."

What are they waiting for?
Unless it is for the angels to come to them?
Or that the Lord come,
Or that a sign of the Lord come?

And her desire is granted. Her womb, rekindled by her hopes, her woven fibers of blood and flesh, forms a fertile ground awaiting the sperm, a ground ready to make life grow, to give birth to hope. There has been an explosion there in the womb, in her vital parts, which have avidly swallowed the selected, the chosen seed, the only one acceptable, the only one among the hundreds of others, the only one to attach itself, the only one which can penetrate, the only one to shape that unique moment of the creation of a being, the only single one which can form the elements of new life. Oh, the fragility and the beauty of that instant of transformation and blossoming.

Outside, the women stir about the court. Their veils tremble in the wind. It is the *khamsin*, the desert wind, which has been blowing for several days and will blow for three, five, or seven more, sweeping along sand and more sand everywhere. The sand infiltrates beneath the veils and into the most hidden creases. And the women groan. They slosh pails of water in the court and the children are stopped from their playing, immobilized by the heat.

E. also suffers from the heat. She is stretched out on her bed, throat parched, eyelids heavy with sand. She asks for something to drink.

God knows what every woman endures, the duration of gestation.
everything is measured by it.
Within her, water will gush forth,
The water which will make green the desert.
We send the winds laden with heavy clouds.
We make fall from the heavens water from which to give
you drink and which you are unable to maintain.

E. does not succeed in believing that. Everything in her seems dried out and she groans and twists about on her bed. The women bring her lemonade scented with orange blossoms. She tries to eat, but nothing goes down but grains of sand and the hot, moving air which kills life.

But where is P.? She no longer sees him. Since she has become pregnant, he neglects her. It is said he is in town. People whisper around her. She picks up bits of phrases which do not surprise her, but sicken her.

Marry as it pleases you—two, three, or four wives.
But if you fear to be unjust, take only one woman or your
captives of war . . .

Now that she no longer serves to satisfy his nightly ardors, now that he has sown his seed and the seed has taken hold and she is confined to her bed, ill fron the heat and fear for the new life she feels in her, he lets her alone. He goes elsewhere now. Shouldn't she be relieved for that? Why the fear?

The term of waiting for pregnant women will end with the birthing.

Allah makes things easy for those who fear Him.

She feels terribly alone in the Damascene room in the violet-colored bed. It's worse than the room of the nailed shutters and double-locked door, for there is nothing outside of it. There is not even the sea with the infinite horizons.

And her womb takes on size and expands as do the flowers of the desert which open in a single day into large, brilliantly colored petals which live only a single day. She looks at her smooth abdomen, watching the tremblings of the skin when the child inside turns. She drinks a lot, she drinks all the time. She would like the water to replenish her and create in her a new life, a different kind of life, a child who will cry out that which she had to hold silent. It is needful that it, the child, speak, that at least it, the child, communicate that vision absorbed by silence.

—They want me to accept, to be quiet, to stifle the revolt in me: well I shall cry it out through the child. I will pass on to the child that breath which they want me to stifle.

And E. drinks, and she eats some dates. May this water, may this fruit, weave in her a real life, a life which will cry out for justice, truth, and liberty.

The child will leave the tent for the desert
The child will search the way of the river
The child will light the flowers of flame
The child will give to birds the seeds of sunlight.

And the wind will sweep all away
And the dust will rise, blinding the child, desiccating fruits and flowers
And the child will follow the river down to the sea.
It will cry out against its mother who gave it birth.

The man returns not. The man stays in the town which feeds his wishes, his ambitions, his pride, his own self-love.
The man runs to business, to money, to women whom he buys with his prestige and his power.

56

Woman, rise up from behind your veil.
Woman, refuse this empire over you,
This force which brings you to nothing.
Woman, make heard your voice which is but the start of a tremor,
Because, for the moment, your voice is like the violin of the desert nights.
It must unite with all the other voices from veils,
With other hands of mornings,
And may all those hands and all those voices take the swords, and turn them into roses, into fertile soils, and into gardens.

The house of packed earth drinks in the sun and does not cast it back. It is hot, a heat which breathes of fear and incarceration. E. keeps herself in the courtyard, withdrawn into herself. Flies light upon her and she lacks the strength to chase them away. They fly about everywhere, alighting on the mouths, on the eyes, of children: everywhere flies, large shaggy flies, tiny flies with busy legs, blue flies, red flies, and black flies—a carpet of flies, a veil of flies.

In the courtyard the women busy themselves with the little girls who are being prepared for excision. There are three between the ages of ten and twelve who stand at the center, eyes cast down, hands folded across their abdomens, eyes lined with kohl, hands and feet tinted with henna, faces whitened with powder and cheeks rubbed with rouge, their dresses spangled and sparkling with white and gold. The midwife enters the court, followed by other women and members of the family of the young victims. Her arms are covered with bracelets of gold, her hair twisted with henna, shines under a multicolored fichu. Her forehead is tatooed and her scant-toothed mouth shows some spots of gold.

And the girls tremble in the courtyard. Often they have been menaced about the excison when they were quite little: "If you do such and such you will be excised and if you do so and so, you will be taken to the doctor for a shot." But these were but threats, now they are here facing an operation whose extent they understand but vaguely. They have heard neighbors of their ages who have howled for days and nights and they know that blood will flow.

Blood scares them
The blood of henna
The blood of women
The blood which runs along the earth
The blood which turns the land into gardens of fear and
violence
The blood of the throat-slashed lamb
Tears of blood which flood the plains
The women who follow one by one unconcious of the
excision
Unconcious of the knife
Unconcious of the vise
Unconcious of the stop put to their ecstacy.

And the little girls tremble in the courtyard. And the wind blows in the enclosure, lifting sand, carrying flies, flies which stick to eyes and mouths of children, flies waiting for the blood. The women have spread out a matting. They bring the water in basins, and incense which they burn in earthen pots. The midwife has squatted down. She draws out her instruments from a large piece of red cloth stained with oily splotches: a pointed knife, razor blades, polished stones, green henna powder, bits of thread, needles.

Knife of the sacrifice
The cutting blade which kills, which separates, which tears
out
the nipples of desire
the petals of joy
the opening to ecstasy.
Closed, sewn up, sealed for ever
Like a great veil of iron
Like a rusty mask
Like a curtain of iron.

Now the women have seized the first little girl. They hold her on all sides. They lift up her gown and make her sit down on a stool which overhangs a white basin. They draw apart her legs and expose her shaved pubic area with the sex glowing in the sunlight. The little girl's attention is fixed as if hypnotic. The midwife parts the large labia and the minor labia. She forces the clitoris, which has been prepared by months of rubbing it with irritants, to protrude. And the witch-woman cuts off the clitoris and tosses it into the basin. The girl howls with pain. And the blood flows. The women hold the little one more firmly. The witch continues her work of mutilation. She cuts away the large labia, like large ears red with fear, and they join the clitoris in the basin. The blood flows heavily now and the shrieks of the girl are like those of a dog whose throat is being slit. The other little girls are shaken with tremblings, but their faces are frozen. They have been prepared for months also. They know they have to pass through all this to become women, that they will not be able to be married if they have not been cut and sewn, and that they must not show that they are afraid if they wish to be thought of as women and no longer as children. And the witch completes her massacre. The minor labia have also been cut away and leveled. The sex which should be smooth and clean, without masculine ambiguity, is but a gaping wound, bloated and bloody. And the blood flows over the legs and the gown of the little girl who screams. And the women call and chant, scanning a rhythm. And the chants drown out the cries of the child. The women chant their revenge.

Mutilated innocents!
Women cry out in the plains
Women chant in the enclosure
Remembering the same knife
Of the same assassin, the same blood
And the child bewails the suffering
Of the bird, dead at the crossroads.

And E. looks upon the scene with terror. The child in her womb has moved. She places her hands upon her abdomen and tries to quiet that life already manifest inside her. That life which will cry in coming forth, and which should proclaim a new way. But she is frightened. What if the child is a girl? And what if she too should come under the knife which mutilates, which enslaves, which suffocates? What if that life should be crushed out, even before having been able to know the dew of mornings and the fragrance of nights?

Flies cling to her. They fly from the basins filled with sacrificial blood and flesh to her hands, to her abdomen, to her head. Their legs, sticky with fresh blood, work avidly at the swelling of her abdomen. She is seized with disgust. She rises, and teetering on her legs, goes back to her room. She barely has time to lean over a bowl before she vomits all she has. She vomits the blood and she vomits fear. She vomits the sacrficial flesh and she vomits the disgust of having to be what she is, a woman bent in half, who can only genuflect before her Lord and Master, before the Father-all-Powerful, before all the P.'s of this world.

And the woman vomits her grief
And spits out the oppobrium of her lack of power
She gives back to the earth the blood of her mutilation
She spits out her anguish and disgust
She throws up from her bowels her bitterness
And bile mounts, mounts and blinds her. The sour taste of
the poison which fills her gushes out and runs over the
ground, which absorbs it. She kneels on the rug, prostrated,
bent double. She holds her womb which has not emptied.
She calms herself very slowly.

Outdoors, the little girls continue to howl. The women chant and scan the rhythms to drown the howlings of these young ones from whom they have cut the life, from whom they have just cut the quiverings of joy, the exchange of amorous glances, the appeal of shared desire, the voice of the beloved, the gift and request expressed without fear or restraint, the intoxication of the ecstasy of two in love performing different acts which harmonize to make a common song:

A common light
A victory fed in love
A freedom woven of tenderness
An equality which respects the differences of each and other.

E. begins again to vomit. She stops her ears so as to hear no more of the howlings which echo in the depths of her own self and which wound her in all her inner being, which mutilate in herself her softness, her goodness, her perseverance, her honesty, and her love—qualities she tries to cultivate in spite of the hatred and rage which surround her. She presses her hands against her ears and she spits into the basin and wails as she spits.

She cries out against customs which transform to demean
Cries out against women who mangle their daughters
Cries out against men who extol the virgin
Against men who require an *excisée*.
Against men who require the vagina sewed and puffed with blood.

And E. weeps for her lack of power. She weeps for her feebleness in face of the violence and the carnage which she can't stop. She weeps not to be able to use her tears to save her child, to save all girls and all the children one prepares for a life of blood. How to revolutionize a world which perpetuates violence and war under a pretext of revolution? How to stop that mutilation before it brings on others? How:

To take my tears to wash away the blood
To take my hands to halt the knife
To take my voice to force a new song to be heard above the
howling
To take the bird and give it space in a sky harmonious and
blue
To take the tree and plant it in the desert near the
bird?

An odor of burning incense reaches her. The little girls seem
somewhat calmed. Stumbling, she crosses the doorsill and observes the
spectacle. The little girls are bedded on the ground in pools of blood.
On every side there are earthen pots giving off smoke. It is a very strong
incense which burns a mixture of aloe, benzoin, and sandalwood. The
witch is squatting down, applying egg yolk and green henna to the still-
bleeding wounds. A procession is forming. The mothers hold the basins
containing the clitorides and vaginal labia of their daughters. They
chant and scan a rhythm:
—Bring them now a husband . . . They are ready. Let them receive
a penis now; they are women.

When the land shall be violently shaken
When the mountains shall be made to move
And then become a dust, spread wide

In the gardens of delight
There will be many men among the first to come
And a few among the last
Placed side by side on beds of ease
They will recline on elbows, face to face

There will be there Houris with large eyes
Like hidden pearls
As payment for their deeds

It is we, in truth, who made these Houris
In perfect form
We have made them virgins
loving and of matchless youth
as companions of the just.

And the procession moves along chanting in the direction of the river. E. hesitates. She stumbles, she fears she cannot go the distance. She studies the young girls who look half dead stretched out on mats, bathed in their own blood. She must understand. She must follow the procession to its end and see. She holds her hands against her abdomen. She feels heavy and alone. One little girl opens her eyes and watches her. The look pierces E. through. She has seen that look elsewhere. She recognizes that sadness and those questions, that anguish and that suffering . . . the young woman on the boat. The young Egyptian who had described this scene to her, only to disappear thereafter. E. find's her here once again. E. moves toward that girl-child and smiles to her. But the girl has already closed her eyes in a grimace of pain. E. looks at the gaping vulva, bleeding in spite of the application of henna. E. fears she shall be ill again. She runs, runs far from that spectacle, far from that girl, a slashed bird reminding her of that other mutilated woman from the past. She runs across the sands, falling down, several times, on her knees; getting up to run again, sobbing from all the griefs she flees.

E. rejoins the procession. The women are at the shore of the river. They hold the basins above their heads and recite the Koran, swaying from right to left. Their ritual gowns of many colors are spangled with silver and gold, and their jewels of gold sparkle in the sun. Their large black veils puff out in the wind and with their chanting.

O, Prophet!
When the believing women come to you
And swear allegiance to you
All the while swearing
That they will hold nothing above God
That they will not steal
That they will not yield themselves in adultery
That they will not slay their own children
That they will commit no infamous act
Neither by hand nor by foot
That they will not disobey that which is correct
Receive their oath of allegiance
Ask pardon of God for them
—God is he who pardons. He is merciful.

And the mothers cast the contents of the basins into the river. For an instant, the water takes on a reddish color, but all disappears beneath the green reflection of the river.

E. regards her image reflected in the water, a mirror of her past life, a vision of the future. She shudders at the aspect of that woman with the swollen abdomen, the great, dark, sad eyes, the hands reaching out toward the horizon in an attitude of challenge and prayer. Her whole silhouette is shown there in the water, deep and green.

The women have departed and E. follows them at a distance. She feels very weary and feeble. Night is falling. The desert takes on a tint of violet and blue. The dunes of sand stand as great shadows, sinister and cold. The coutryard is also cold and gloomy. The court is filled with women. On one side there are those who tie the legs of the little girls, who look like corpses, mummies well bound; and on another side, women unroll the rug-mats. Still other women enter with offerings of dates, perfume and incense.

Coffee urns and tea caddies hiss above the charcoal. Two of the little girls have again begun to cry. How many times will they have to endure this suffering? Will she have the strength to bear it? E. falls in a corner of the court. A woman brings her some tea which she flavors with orange blossoms. Usually, she likes that odor and those of other beverages like coffee and flavored with cardamon. But today an insurmountable nausea has taken possession of her and will not leave her. She drags herself, creeps along, to her room, takes a sleeping pill, plugs her ears with cotton to stop hearing those cries.

The little child awakens from a long slumber
He runs toward the sands
He runs along the river road
He approaches the large and sour plants
He contemplates the colored rocks
The river watches him
And the child approaches it with wonder
He opens wide his arms toward the strand
He calls, calls out with all his might
A vessel shows its outline against the horizon
At the bottom of the vessel there is a box
And the child cries out and waves his arms
The vessel advances on the waters
The child walks along the river
In the direction of the vessel
In the direction of the sea

And the dragon sees him from the depths of the stream
And the dragon, annoyed with woman and child,
Rises up in all his might to the surface of the water
And with a flick of his mouth, he swallows the child
And the dragon, satiated and appeased, turns toward the
sea
He will sit upon the golden sands, stirring his serpent-long
tail with the scales shining in the sun.

The next morning E. awakes, feeble and with a bitter, acidulous taste in her mouth. She places her hands upon her abdomen. The baby has moved. She tries to get up, but falls back with weakness upon the mattress. Where is he who should help her? He who should carry her and move her in moments like these when her legs refuse to support her? She notices, through the half-opened door, the sunlight which floods the land. He will not return until the baby is born. Perhaps the child will not be born. Perhaps he will never return at all.

To create a new man
A man capable of tenderness, not a schemer
A man whose wisdom will no longer stand as
Forces of destruction and of power
But as forces of love and generosity
To construct him slowly, silently
With tremendous patience and a will to triumph over his
destructive violence
So that the better self in him shall speak.

A man for trees, a man for roots
A man for cedars, a man for branches
A man for nests, a man for birds
A man for worlds new found.

Lebanon, rebuilt by the new man
Lebanon, stretching out her millenial branches,
New grown and nourishing the world
Lebanon of trunks and fruits
Lebanon of new-found starry nights
Lebanon of hills reforested
Lebanon of voices harsh now purified
Lebanon of children brought back to life.

Lebanon of trees, Lebanon of youth
Lebanon of seeds and gardens.

She drags herself along in the, now empty, courtyard. There is only sunlight, sunlight everywhere, sunlight on the stone and sunlight on the sand. Flies buzz here and there, near whatever retains traces of blood. They attack her precipitately, her gown and veil soiled from the night before. E. raises her hands to her forehead. She can hardly breathe under the veil, under the mask. A little girl, not yet excised, approaches her and smiles. She is holding in her hands some dates which she offers E. The dates are covered with flies. E. refuses. She caresses the head of the little girl who watches her with wide, questioning eyes.

E. takes her hand and draws her toward one of the doors which opens to the interior. The room she sees is engagingly shady and fresh. Inside, one of the excised girls is stretched out on a mat, her legs tied. She groans, her mouth is rigid with pain. Her hands, stained with henna, twist nervously above her head. She breathes and groans in spasms. E. approaches her and strokes her head and hands as if to give courage. She is the little girl who had watched E. the night before. Her aspect is sad and resigned, with a glint from time to time of revolt, quickly abandoned, and the rictus of her mouth accentuated.

E. sits on the ground with the women who are drinking coffee and eating dates. To them everything appears normal: the little girls excised, the river appeased by the mutilated sex organs, the blood in the enclosure, and the blood running now, the wounds which are going to stick to one another to close up the sex passage which will be brutally opened twice on the wedding night—with a knife, she has been told. But truly, do these women accept such customs? For they suffer; the suffering can be read in their eyes, above all in the eyes of the younger ones. E. approaches one of them to talk with her, to try to understand, to try to lift the veil.

—You were there yesterday at the time of the Excison?

—Yes. I saw you—you left and went back to your room. Did you feel ill?

—Yes. I can't bear the sight of blood, and I don't understand this operation. Why? Why cut those little girls?

—It's tradition. Men wouldn't marry them else. They would not be accepted if they were not excised. Don't think about it. Don't be so sad.

The young woman watches her with sympathy. Her eyes suggest astonishment mixed with an unbearable sadness. Here there is not the least trace of revolt like that of the Egyptian woman on the boat.

One of the older women in the group, who has heard the conversation, approaches them. She makes an obscene gesture of cutting off the clitoris, and laughs sadistically.

—It has to be, my little one, it has to be. God has decreed it. One must be pure. Circumcision is purification.

And she raises her arms heavenward to Allah, adding:

—Our whole life for us, women, is suffering, pure and simple. God has ordered it.

Khatin, Tahara
cut, but cut not too much
Cut, cut, cut
But
Not
Too, much.
Then close it up and let God weld the whole.
Then cut again, reweld, and cut again.

Allah wishes it
Women excised
Once
Twice
Thrice
Khatin, Tahara, Khatin.

The blows fall like rain upon E. As in her childhood when blows rained down. E. has once revolted. She has already cried out. She has already fled once, thinking to resolve the problems of her childhood, believing that she was going towards something better, towards a goal, with a different kind of man. Filled with hopes, she crossed the sea, the desert. She found a desert, she found a river, a land of dates and palms. But he, what does he seek? And where is he? Where is the box that they were to find together? Time passes, life closes in upon her. No horizon is possible any more. Nothing but a barrier, there at the pit of her stomach, a barrier obstructing her breath. Must one revolt against God in order to break these chains which even women attribute to God? Must one revolt against the Man and the Father, against all fathers who apply the precepts of Pater-Omnipotent? Or should one, on the contrary, go to them, go to Him, and see if, rather, it is not that man has travestied His Image? She has already rebelled once. She has already crossed the sea one time. What must now be done? Must one revolt continuously, indefinitely? And how can she now rebel? Where to turn? What to do? And what good is a revolt, if all the other women do not rebel with her? The case of the young Egyptian on the boat returns to her mind. An isolated case? How many others like it are there? How to take all the women and make of them a solid chain which will break all these other chains? What about the brothers armed with poignards who follow to cut their throats? And what of the whole background society which presses the brothers to slay their sisters to avenge for honor at all costs? She is tired of these questions. When he comes back—if he comes back—ought she not speak to him, to him?

The old woman in the group approaches E. and lifts up her gown:

—Are you excised, you foreign woman? How is that done where you come from? Do you pray to God in the same way we do?

The old woman's bony hands are stained reddish brown with henna. E.'s stomach turns with revulsion. She snatches the gown from the hands of the old woman. She watches the group. All the women are smiling behind their masks. They come towards her hands extended to lift her gown and look. E. is seized with panic. With fright she watches the women, a sea of fury, a wave ready to submerge her, to drown her, to wipe out her differences. She recoils toward the door, her heart beating as if to burst, her hands moist, her face contracted behind the mask which stifles her. She barely has enough time to rush outside and flee. She runs to her room, closes the door and braces a chair and a table against it to prevent its opening. Her heart beats furiously. How to protect herself? How to defend herself agaist these women who seem to thirst for blood and bleeding organs of sex? She is fearful. What to do? Where to go? Will they enter and tie her up also? Why such rage against her differences? Her entire insides ache. Her whole body cries out.

She looks about her. How to escape? Where to flee? There is a back window. But could she get up through it and then climb the wall which surrounds the courtyard? She totters. Will she have enough strength to leave? And where to go?

    To follow the way of the river
    Find again the sea
    Climb the mountains
    Take the little babe toward the ship
    To give the chance of another life
    Show it the horizon lit by the sun

And take the blood from the river
And take the corpses from the sea
To plant the desert and water it
Until a new woman
Until a new man put forth roots and branches and
leaves
Which will transform the world.

Outside, the women have quieted. E. hears only the sobbing of a girl excised the night before. Night falls rapidly as it does in the desert, instantly refreshing. Suddenly there is a knock at the door.

—Who is it? E. asks.

—Open, open up, cries P. Why have you barricaded yourself now?

E. comes forward, trembling, and half-opens the door. He pushes it brutally. He is there before her and she hardly recognizes him; he is so changed. He is heavier and his features have thickened. He has assumed the manner of a man who believes himself important.

—Why are you locking yourself in?

She must speak with him. She must cry out her disillusions and her fears. She must try to explain it to him.

—Listen. I can't stand it any more. I don't recognize you. Where is our dream? Where is all that we were going to realize together when mouth to mouth on the sands of my country, stretched out on the shore, you promised me that we were going to build a new, different world, you and I?

—What do you want me to do? Tie myself up with you like the Western men do? Your place is here among the women. It is here you must work. I, I work outside with men, in the city. It is there that I must try to improve the state of my people.

—But don't you see what you have become? Look at yourself a moment. Do you know what women of this country do to other women? They mutilate them, they cut them. They tear out the most delicate and most precious and important sexual parts.

He sneers.

—That's tradition. You ought not to have come here if you were so squeamish.

—Tradition. Tradition. But weren't we coming here to change traditions? So that a woman would rise up side by side with a man? Ought not we display a different image of man and wife?

— The married couple—that's a Western idea. It has no place in the Arab world. When will you understand that the Arab world is Islam

69

and Islam is the Arab world?

—No, no, no! I am Christian and an Arab, Arab and Christian. I am also a woman, above all a woman, and I want to live. And I want you and me to be different, to give others an example. Listen to me, hear me well. Don't you want us to find again, you and I together, that magic box of your childhood?

She has approached him with all her body, her expression, her hands, her flesh can communicate to him of tenderness and of desire for communication. He looks at her fixedly for a moment, his attitude surly. At the mention of the box, he started, his looks unguarded as in days past. For a moment, she thinks she touched the sensitive chord in him, the chord which will allow them to begin once more, to find each other again, to change things. She moves still closer to him and places her hands on his shoulders. She strokes his back softly to soothe him, to cradle him, to soften him and make him become again what he was before when, in front of his class of Palestinian children, he had told the story which lighted flames of hope in the eyes of the children and when his ardent look had lighted a flame of love in her heart. But his muscles tense under her fingers and his body is like a bundle of iron knots. His forehead creases and furrows. Sweat stands out on his temples and slips along his cheeks, puffy and red. His breath is heavy and charged with alcohol and the words which he casts forth at her face strike her and make her recoil to a corner of the room where she feels herself sinking in new despair. He sneers:

—The box of my childhood . . . how could you ever believe in such a story? You really are most naïve. When will you learn that the world is not created from dreams and illusions, but from facts with numbers and with money?

—No. No, you are wrong. The most beautiful worlds, the best and truest ones, are made because of dreams and because of visions. I reject your theories and I reject your way of imprisoning me. If you do not give back to me my freedom, I shall take it. You will never again see me.

E. stands up to him as she ought to have done long before, as she ought to have done to her father in her youth. Yes, there's where she ought to have affirmed herself. But it is not too late. She must seize the initiative. She must rise up and show that she exists right now. She must make her voice heard, for the sake of the women around her and for all women in the world who are waiting, who will understand, perhaps, and will follow her, perhaps, and will stir and lift themselves up, perhaps.

But she has gone too far. P. looks at her with hate and scorn, sure of his strength and his omnipotence, sure of his might and his values. He brandishes a chair at her and moves angrily toward her. Her heart pounds. Is he going to kill her? Will she no longer have anything to fear in just a few moments? Crushed and annihilated, will she pass the threshold of death, will she have come to the end of all her suffering and all her despair, of all her struggles and all her revolts?

But he drops the chair. His blood-shot eyes cloud over. He sneers again and falls in a lump on the bed. She looks at that man she has followed thinking that with him, together, they would be able to march toward the light.

Formless mass of tangled snares
Man has brandished his dagger
He whets his knives in the light of the city
He makes the blade shine in the morn of day
He walks on the flowers, scarcely opened in deserts
mute
He thinks he understands the woman under the veil
Since he has locked her into an enclosure
Since he has closed the doors
Since he has walled in the gardens,
And when a woman lifts herself up
He strikes her down
And when a woman speaks a word
He nails shut her mouth
And when a woman looks at him
He runs away
And the town wraps itself around, enclosing him.

When you ask anything
Of the wives of the prophet
Ask it behind the veil
That is the most chaste way for your hearts and for their
hearts.

O, Prophet
Tell your wives, and your daughters
And all wives of all believers
To cover themselves with veils!
That is for them the best way
To make themselves known
And to not be offensive.
—God is the one who pardons
He is merciful.

E. has sunk down in a corner. She weeps, at first softly, then with more and more force. She bewails her impotence, her feebleness, her inability to communicate to him that with all her body, all her flesh, all her tenderness, all her love she wants to make him live. Suddenly she feels a hand placed upon her head. It is the little girl of the morning, the little girl who had offered her the dates covered with flies. E. looks at her through her tears. It is the little child of hope who looks at her with tenderness and whose eyes communicate a sweetness and a freshness of childhood.

—I must leave this place, E. tells her. Would you like to come away with me?

—Where are you going? the little girl asks.

—Towards the river, towards the sea.

The little girl smiles to her and acquiesces with a nod of her head.

—I'll be back at once, she says with exuberance.

E. rapidly gathers some things into a red foulard: her jewels of gold, bracelets, earrings in the shape of twigs, a brooch shaped like a bird, some pendants, necklaces, rings. Some of her most precious books: *The Sixth Day*, *Return Home*, *The Sun and the Earth*, *The Wretched*, *The Statue*, *People*, *Nefertiti and the Dream of Akhnaton*, *The Third Voice*, *The Last Song*, *From Sleep Unbound*, and a notebook of addresses.

The little girl returns carrying a basket too, full of dates and bananas. In a corner of the basket there is a metal box.

—That's halewa, she says, indicating the box.

E. smiles happy with the thought.

—Come, she says. We must leave before dawn.

E. takes the little girl's hand. She glances at P. who sleeps and snores with an open mouth.

—Come, let's go.

They cross the enclosure, which is deserted and dark. There are no flies. From time to time a mosquito approaches, buzzing. The little girl squeezes E.'s hand with confidence. In the distance a cock crows. Dawn is near. The desert night is fresh. Silently and with cat steps they cross the courtyard. They open the door of the enclosure which happily is not locked. Hopefully, the door through the wall which surrounds the enclosure and the houses will also be open. E.'s heart pounds. The door lightly squeaks and E. looks about on all sides, but all is dark and silent. Trees rustle in the breeze. The second door is locked! It is of iron, forged with Islamic motifs.

—We will have to climb over, E. says to the little girl. Go on up,

The little girl is quite agile. She puts her basket at the base of the

72

wall and climbs up like a young monkey. A snake comes out of its hole and glides toward the basket. E. shudders. Dawn is breaking and the cock crows a second time. They must hurry. The women are going to begin to emerge. The snake glides along the wall and enters the court-yard. E. passes the basket and the laden foulard to the little girl who now bestrides the top of the wall. E. begins to climb as well, with the help of the Islamic motifs which serve as foot-holds. But she has neither the youth nor the strength of the little girl, and her long gown and her veil hinder her. The child she is carrying in her womb is heavy and she fears to stumble.

—We'll make it, she says. We'll get there. We've got to reach the river.

The little child must see the sea. She holds onto the iron figures and pulls herself slowly up the door. The little girl smiles and holds out her hands. Now E. is also atop the wall and she watches along with the little girl as the snake sips water from the basin in the center of the court. The cock crows a third time and they hear sounds in some of the buildings.

—We must hasten, E. says to the little girl. Go down slowly and I will hand you the basket and the foulard.

—No, you first, says the little girl.

She sees that E. has trouble keeping her balance on top of the wall.

—You first; go down slowly. It's not hard, there is sand at the bottom—even if you fall, you won't hurt yourself. I'll take care of things. Go!

It is she who gives the orders. It is the little girl who has taken matters in hand, as if she felt that, thanks to her, thanks to her determination and to her courage, E. would accomplish the task.

She is the little girl of hope.
Who smiles and who conveys the strength and tender-
ness
The little girl of dates and halewa
Far away from the guns and engines of death.
The little girl of the desert, and of cacti
She is the sunshine, she is the light
The little girl of trees which flower
And of the bird who sings.

E. lets herself slowly down the door. Her gown and her veil are of light cloth which snags on the Islamic motifs. She is afraid they will rip, and she descends with great precaution. Her hands are bruised and bluish, her face stretched with fright. The little girl encourages her.

—You're almost down. Let yourself fall now. It is sandy, you won't hurt yourself.

E. sprawls on the sand. Her gown and her veil are torn in many places. She looks upward. The little girl holds out the basket and the foulard. E. has just time enough to grasp them. The little girl is already down.

—We must go quickly, the girl says. We must run. I fear a woman has seen me.

They hold hands and they run; they run through the sand, across the dunes, through sand still cool with the freshnes of the night, through sand still damp with the dew of the morning. The little girl seems to know the way to the river. It is she who leads. It is she who directs and shows where to go. Instinct presses her towards the sunlight, towards the river. And E. lets herself be guided. Along the horizon the sky is rosy. Morning begins and with it, heat emanates from rocks and bushes. Low on the ground, a moist fog rises, rises and moves. E. feels heavy and winded. She follows the little girl with difficulty who leaps forth like a gazelle.

—We're getting there, the girl says. I see the river. I see the sunlight.

—What is your name? E. asks. You have not told me your name.

—I am called Nour.

—Nour, my light, my sunshine, you are my life, says E., taking the little girl into her arms and stopping at the margin of a dune.

—Come. Let's stop here a moment and eat some dates. We must fortify ourselves. A long journey is ahead of us.

They sit upon the sand. Nour opens the metal box.

—It's some halewa from the excision, she says. My sister received several boxes like this one. Mama had hidden them, but I knew where they were. Here, she says, and offers E. a crispy piece redolent of honey and orange blossoms, with a sweetness which melts against the palate.

—What a good idea you had, says E. It's food from heaven.

—It's also food for birds, says Nour. Look!

She holds out her hand on which rest a few crumbs. A red bird of paradise comes to peck at these remains of the piece of halewa.

—He didn't peck my hand. Look! He has taken only the crumbs, Nour licks her fingers still sticky with sugar and sesame oil.

—We have to find a boat to take us as far as the town, says E. A

74

boat to take us to the big ship which will take you across the sea.

—And you? asks Nour.

—I, I shall go with you as far as the sea, until you are safe on the large ship which will take you to the country where I shall tell you where to go. But I must return, the river and the desert await me.

Nour says nothing. All at once, her face has become quite sad, with the sadness of a flower which bends down in the sand. Her face has taken on the look of her excised sister, and it passes like a veil of suffering between the two, who have become silent. They look to the river shining in the distance. The red bird of paradise has flown off in the direction of the sea. Nour closes the box which she places in the basket.

—Are there dates there, in the country where I must go?

—No, there are no dates, but there are mountains with high peaks, with eternal snow, with ice which never melts. There is no halewa, but there is chocolate, very good chocolate.

—And are there birds?

—Yes, there are many birds and there are trees which you don't know of and which are very beautiful and always green. They are called evergreens.

But the face of Nour is still sad. She gets up abruptly, shakes the crumbs from her gown, and takes E.'s hand. They turn in silence toward the river.

They see in the distance a little boat which shines in the morning sun. The fog is dissipating over the river which appears motionless and mysterious. They wave, making large signals. The boat approaches. A sad and langorous melody reaches them in snatches. It is a melody from E.'s adolescence, one of the melodies heard on the cliff roads of her country when, hand in hand with P., they had made plans for the future, plans of hope—where, together, they had sketched out the flowers of passion and the tree of life which would renew the world. The melody becomes more and more distinct. It is the boatman who sings while rowing.

Woman of sunlight
Go, find again your lover of fruits and roots
He awaits you where the sun never sets.
Woman of sunlight
Go toward the horizon purpled by the sea
Write your name in stardust
Cling to the wings of heaven.

75

Woman of sunlight
Trace a road in the desert
Follow the swallow which flies toward the light
And find again the voice of the wind.
O-o-oh, you woman of sunlight and dreams.

The boat is very near to them. E. approaches the boatman.
—We are on our way to V City. can you take us there?
She takes out several bracelets and a brooch in the form of a fish.
The jewels shine brightly in the light of the risen sun. The boatman
religiously accepts the offering and signals them to step up. He helps
them climb into the boat. Nour seems to have lost her eagerness for
departure and she clings to E. mewling.
—Come, my dear, says E. to her. You are tired. Come, sleep in my
arms till we reach town, till the next boat. Sleep, my life, sleep, my
soul. You'll need your strength. You'll need much courage to persevere
and reach where you must go.
E. has enfolded Nour in her veil and has seated herself in a corner
of the boat, caressing and cradling the child. The boatman has resumed
his oars and his song.

She was born for the stars
For the breath which runs through her
She was born for the voyage
Over land and skies and seas.
She remains now alone and broken
She knows no place to go.
She has reached the sea
And the sea has accepted her.

She was born to blossom
To receive the fruits of life.
She was born to rush headlong
Toward the horizon, toward harvests, toward song.
She remains now alone and broken
She knows no place to go.
She has walked to the edge of the river
And the river has accepted her.

E. watches the green reflection which the sunlight paints over with gold and siver. What strength! What peace! What tranquility of shores which contemplate each other, and of a world which flows and vibrates under the light of the sun. Little by little, the city shows itself in the distance, a town of the desert, a town rose, yellow and gray, surrounded by palm trees and tall minarets—symbols. A town of silence and contemplation. The humidity and heat halo it with a mist and dust. It is the city at the river's mouth, the city of the delta, a city triangular in form, the city of the hated veil. It is a city of fruits which ripen and sun which sucks them dry. How far away is her own town and how far away the stripped banana trees, the dried dates, the blood burning the vines and the grain and the child crying for its wounds and its throat-cut mother.

—Over there is the great port, says the boatman, indicating to them a white jetty in the distance and a calm bay filled with small and large ships, warships and fishing vessels. You must get out here, he continues, and take the road to the right. It runs along the quay and the markets. Follow the river and you'll get there.

E. thanks him and takes Nour by the hand. Nour leans toward the boatman and gives him her basket of bananas, dates and halewa.

—Thank you for your songs, she murmurs.

The boatman smiles, helps them step down and resumes his oars and his song and the direction toward the village, the direction of all that they have fled. The melody is sad and langorous. It flows with the boat over the river of green and violet tones. E. and Nour listen, seized by the beauty and the magic of the words and the sounds, hypnotized by the motion of the distancing boat and of the song which envelops them and finds them even from afar by the force of echo.

> Layla with skin the color of night
> Layla with eyes wet with tears
> She has knocked at closed doors
> She has broken through frozen walls
> She has sketched in herself for herself
> A way filled with stars
> She has run toward the forest
> She has fed all the birds.
>
> She was born for the stars
> For the breath which runs through her
> She was born for the voyage
> Over land and skies and seas
> She remains now alone and broken

She knows no place to go.
She has reached the sea
And. . . .

Nour shudders and clings to E. They move on, hand in hand, through narrow streets filled with merchants, stores cafés: alleys with the smell of garlic, oil, fish, and fried foods.

—I would love to eat a large fish like that one, says Nour, pointing to a sole, delicate and oval, finely ribbed and golden.

—We shall eat some, I promise you, my dear one. We shall eat a large fish like that one just as soon as we have bought the ticket. Come, let us not delay.

There is hardly a woman in the marketplace, for it is the men who make the purchases and E. fears that she will be singled out. Already, men are looking at Nour with obscene intensity. Happily, she herself is masked and veiled. She doubles the pace and her veil puffs out like a great black bird. The salt air from the sea lashes her face. Nour has trouble keeping up with her.

—How fast you are going, she says. I don't walk very well except in the sands.

—You'll learn quickly, my life, you shall see. You will learn to run over stones and you will learn to ride in machines which go fast, and one day, you will take flight on a great bird of steel and fly through the skies. You will learn these things, for you are the hope and the light.

—Oh, yes, I shall fly like the birds, Nour murmurs.

They have reached the port. A great white packet boat rises before them. It shows in freshly painted green letters the name, *Hope*.

—That is our fortune, our happiness. It is the ship of hope and life rediscovered, says E.

They approach a ticket counter where two men are talking in Arabic. E. hesitates. Should she speak to them? An instinct tells her no, there is danger. She withdraws and walks along the quay. Great cranes are hoisting crates and vehicles. The dock is at the mouth of the river against the sea. The air sticks to one's skin. How to find a means of getting Nour on board? E. looks about her on all sides. Behind the grillwork, people are waiting to board. E. sees two children seated on valises. They hold in hand a cage of parakeets. Suddenly, a woman appears in the crowd who makes E.'s heart leap. It is a woman E. has seen before: the appearance of freedom, the slight figure, the brown hair, the sad glance; the determination and pride mixed with sweetness. *It is that woman.*

78

—All's ready, says the woman to the two children. We can board now, the ship leaves in three hours.

—I'm hungry, says the little boy. You promised us fish.

E. approaches them:

—May I invite you to eat fish? My daughter is dying for some also.

At the sound of her voice, the woman trembles. She looks at the speaker, veiled and masked, who has approached them, and falls back a step, surprised. E. lifts her mask and looks at her. The two women stare at each other and a world of understanding and communication flows between them in that moment, drawing them together once more.

—Come, says the woman, let's find a quiet place where we can watch our baggage and eat tranquilly.

Not far from them, is a sort of a café-restaurant with a mauve façade, a court filled with tables and with trees spreading shade and freshness. In the center of the court there is a reflecting pool. It is a pleasant spot and they approach it, drawn by the odors of coffee, fish, and frying foods.

—Sit there, the woman tells E. You will be behind the tree, and you can remove your mask. The children can watch the baggage.

E. removes her mask and her veil. She breathes deeply. The woman has taken out a pack of cigarettes. She extends the pack toward E., who hesitates. E. has not smoked since that voyage when she first encountered her, the Egyptian on the boat.

—Take one. Smoke, urges the woman. It will relax you. You seem to be very tense.

The two women are in rapport and they smoke in silence. They look at each other with understanding. It is an entire world which speaks across their exchanged glances through the veil of cigarette smoke, a world of suffering and oppression, a world of silence and acceptance, a world of revolt and overturnings, of movement toward life and freedom.

—I want sole, says Nour, the fish we saw at the entrance to the port, the flat and oval fish.

—Yes, me too, says the boy. And I want it fried with tartar sauce.

The two women smile at the enthusiasm of the children. The Egyptian orders the fish. E. takes out her foulard which she hands to the Egyptian.

—Here are my jewels, my papers, and an address book. I have underlined names and addresses where Nour will be able to go.

—Don't worry about it, says the Egyptian, taking the foulard and pressing E.'s hands in her own. Nour will be safe. She will reach the country you have described to me. She will cross the seas and find

79

mountains. She will be able, she at least, perhaps to live.

The children babble while eating and laugh. E. looks at the woman, the children, the sea. She is not able to swallow what she has on her plate. A constriction in her throat makes eating impossible. She looks at the ship and the passengers climbing the gangway. Will she at last succeed in coming to the end of her road? And Nour, will she truly find the sunlight? How often must one cross the seas to understand? She wonders.

The Egyptian rises and takes her handbag and the foulard.

—Finish here quietly, she says, I am going to buy another ticket. When I come back, we will have to embark.

E. studies that woman, who resembles her, that woman who goes about in jacket and skirt with a free and easy gait, that woman who is going to leave the desert to regain the mountains. Nour sees that E. is watching the woman and she sees questions and anguish in E.'s eyes. A sudden sadness clouds Nour's vision, but she continues to laugh as she speaks with her new companions who seem enchanted with her. Suddenly, she takes E.'s hand into her own.

—You cannot come with us. I know that you cannot come. But one day, I, I shall return to get you on that great bird you have told me about, that great bird which flies through the skies.

E. smiles at her. The Egyptian has returned with the ticket.

—We must leave now, she says. The ship is going to sail soon.

She shows E. the foulard in which shine several bracelets, the brooch and the earrings:

—There are still enough of the jewels left for the child. She will take precious care of them.

E. replaces her mask and her veil. The woman has called for porters who take charge of the baggage. E. takes Nour in her arms and kisses her. Fortunately, her mask hides her tears and the veil covers her trembling shouders. Nour says nothing. Her gaze is lost in the distance. The Egyptian presses E.'s hand. Their glances meet once more and give them courage. The Egyptian takes her children by the hands; Nour has taken the little boy's hand. E. watches them depart and mount the gangplank. She will not stay to watch the departure of the ship. No longer are their features visible. Already their gestures and the waving of their hands appear far away as though seen through a dense fog. E. again feels a tearing pain within. Her eyes are blurred by tears which she cannot control. She fears making herself conspicuous. Will she be able to carry it all off to the end? She straightens up with courage and daring. She knows where she must go and her steps turn that way, where her reflection is waiting for her, there where her present, past and her future are intertwined at a point which eddies and calls to her. With sure steps, she leaves the port. She feels no fear now. She is going to return to her own center, the culminating point of her existence, the place which the boatman showed her by a wave of his hand when, kneeling in the boat, they approached the town. It was then that he showed her the horizon, the shining spot in the sunlight, the mouth of the river at the sea.

She moves forward with steps sure and firm. She goes through the fish market, the little street encumbered with people, vendors and buyers, which she has crossed a few hours earlier going the opposite way with Nour. The crowd is thicker than before. The sun is at the zenith, and it is very hot. Soon all will be deserted and silent for the siesta. This time the men scarcely look at her and it eases her to be able to walk straight ahead toward her goal.

She arrives at the river's edge, near to the sea. She sees her image reflected in the green waters, an image she has contemplated many a time, understanding the secret call of the flood and the waves. Without the least hesitation, she enters the wave and goes forward toward her image which awaits her. She goes into the waters which close over her. She goes to her rest. She goes to the silence.

The siren emits its lugubrious wail. *The Hope* leaves the quay; soon it will be on the open sea. Nour, leaning against the guard rail, watches the departure of the ship and the waves it makes cutting through the water. Her hair flows in the wind. The Egyptian woman approaches her. The woman lights a cigarette and smokes as she stares at the water. Suddenly, her expression becomes quite sad and she is shaken by sobbing. She nervously drops the cigarette that she had just finished lighting into the sea.

—What's the matter? Nour asks.

—Nothing, says the woman, lighting another cigarette.

In the distance, a boatman rows in the direction of the village. He is singing a sad song and the echo of his song resounds along the river as far as the sea. Nour recognizes the song and she begins softly weeping also.

> She was born for the stars
> For the breath which runs through her
> She was born for the voyage
> Over land and skies and seas
> She remains now alone and broken

She knows no place to go.
She has reached the sea
And the sea has accepted her.

Layla, Layla from the torn-up land
Layla, Layla from the leveled camp
She has drawn breath amid the rubble
She has drawn flowers from the ashes
She has sought in herself, for herself
A different air, another life
She has cried yes to her passion
She has said no to her reason.

She was born to blossom
To receive the fruits of life
She was born to rush headlong
Toward the horizon, toward harvests, toward song
She remains now alone and broken
She knows no place to go
She has walked to the edge of the river
And the river has accepted her.

Layla, Layla, bird of the South
Layla, Layla, jewel of the waters
She has brushed against stone after stone
She has returned a life to the sea
She has drawn alone in the enclosure
A way filled with pictures
She has come alone in the twilight
She has made the opening for all hopes.

Nour has collapsed on the ship's deck. The young woman takes her in her arms and carries her to the cabin. She rubs her, trying to bring life back into the little inert body. She sprinkles her with cold water. Once again she hears from afar the echo of the song upon the sea:

She has loved, she has given

She was born for the stars

She was born for the voyage

She has been broken and mutilated
She has been murdered, she has been slain

She has gone to the edge of the sea
And the sea has accepted her

Nour opens her eyes and sees the young woman who smiles at her.

—You must not let yourself despair. She would have been devastated to see you in this condition, she who counts so much on you to live as she has not been able to live . . . Come, take a sip of water.

The little boy and the little girl have approached the bunk bed and watch Nour who is drinking. Her body is shaken with spasms. Her teeth chatter. The young woman helps her lie back again and wraps her in a shawl.

—Come, she says to the children. Let her rest.

They go to the ship's deck, and the salty air from the sea whips against their faces. The sea is agitated and its whitecaps come breaking with force against the prow. On the horizon, a red sun is on the point of disappearing. The young woman shudders and lights a cigarette. She has to make several tries for the wind blows out the flame.

—I'm hungry, says the little boy.

—You're always hungry answers the little girl.

—Come, let's go in, says the young woman. Let's find the dining room.

The Egyptian looks once more with anguish at the sea. How many times she has crossed it, with always the same anguish in her heart, wondering what she would find at the end of her trip!

The little boy tugs at her sleeve and pulls her away from her thoughts.

—Fortunately, *they* are here, she tells herself. And Nour as well, happily she has been able to get away.

They reach the cabin. Nour is asleep curled up on the bunk bed, wrapped in the shawl. From time to time, her breathing is interrupted with a gasp or a sigh.

—Let her sleep, the woman signs to the children. Tomorrow she will be better.

The next day the sea is more calm. The children run about the deck, laughing. In the distance, the horizon is one of sea, of infinite sea. In a nook on deck the young woman is seated with Nour, who is still wrapped in the shawl. Nour's small face is pale, lined with enormous circles under her eyes. She seems far away, very far, as if rooted in the infinite.

The young woman has lighted a cigarette. She tries to arouse Nour from her torpor.

—You knew her well?

—Oh, no. She was a mystery to everybody. When she arrived at our village, everyone was waiting for her. Her coming had been announced days, even weeks, earlier. Everyone waited with curiosity. I, I too, was curious. And then when I saw her, my feeling of curiosity was transformed into one of affection. There came forth from her such strength and goodness. Even through the mask and the veil her beauty shone . . .

—Yes, her heart was beautiful, her body also for I have seen her unveiled.

—You knew her? Nour sighed.

The young woman hesitated and stayed quiet a long moment before replying. Meanwhile, she had lit another cigarette. She drew in the smoke nervously, deep in thought which seemed sad.

—Yes, several years ago. I made one trip with her. I was fleeing my own country: I was running away from its humiliating customs, which you surely know about. On seeing each other, we felt a sympathy. She told me that she was fleeing her country also, a country at war, and that she also wished to get away from her family which stifled her and imposed upon her values she could never accept. She confided in me and told me that she was going to run away with a man she loved to a distant country . . . a country like the one I had just left.

The woman pauses for a moment. Her forehead is frowning in pain at the memory.

—I told her . . . I told her, however, not to run away. I explained to her the horror of all that I was escaping . . . Oh, why did she not listen to me?

Nour had kept silent during this recall of painful memories, during the evocation of what might perhaps have been prevented. Nour looks at the sea and glances at the woman who has been smoking incessantly since the start of their conversation.

—And how was it that you got away?

—That's a long story. While I was speaking with her, I saw a man in the distance, a man who seemed to be looking for someone. The bearing of that man strangely resembled that of my brother. I was very frightened. For I knew that if my brother had followed me and then found me, he would surely kill me. So I hid myself in the ship's hold. I remained there days and nights in obscurity, shaking with fear. When the ship docked, I waited till everyone got off and then I risked my departure, losing myself in the crowd, running, always running. Every time I saw anyone who resembled my brother, I hid. I was terribly afraid. I was also terribly hungry, for it had been days since I had eaten anything. I had some luck. I come from a well-to-do family. I had jewels which I sold in order to eat and to pass the frontier and hide myself. I was always afraid that my brother might follow my trail by the sold jewels or by that native flair of our men when there is a question of honor . . . It's a long story, but I'll condense it now. I crossed the frontier and found the country to which you and I now are going, and where we will be a few days. Once again, I was lucky to find work with a family of diplomats who wanted me to give lessons in Arabic to their children. Afterwards, I met a man who freed me from my past. I had, I still have a deep love-life with a man who respects me and who has helped me to affirm myself as a whole woman, a total person. My wounds are still there, but they are scarred over now. And I can return to my native country without fear and without bitterness. From time to time, a wound opens again, like yesterday at the moment of my meeting her whom I wish I could have helped. She stands for all those women whom I would love to help scale the walls of shame and despair and put by the veil of silence and oblivion. Fortunately, you are here. I shall help you. It must be for you a bit easier to succeed.

She presses Nour against her. She is silent. Nour is silent as well and weeps softly. Then Nour wipes her tears and drops the shawl as she gets up. Her face shines with understanding and beauty. She stretches her arms toward the sea in a gesture of prayer.

—I wish that she may be proud of me, for she has saved me. Her coming saved me. Thanks to her, I have seen the sunshine and the light. Thanks to her, I shall never wear the stifling mask before my face. Thanks to her, my body will never be sliced like my sister's; surely she is even today crying in pain. I was called Nour at my birth, but without her I would never know the light of day. I must live to help my other sisters. That is what she would have wished, isn't it? Nour asks the young woman.

The woman seems much moved by Nour's declamation. She looks upon the girl whose face is transformed, and who seems suddenly to have matured through several years. She sees in her the beautiful young woman of tomorrow, the young woman who will nourish all hopes.

Epilogue

The summer following, in a house bordering Lake Leman, Nour buries her dead bird. She has placed it in a pretty box she has just painted, a box colored with crosses and crescents, with flowers, with butterflies, and with sunlight. She runs toward the pine forest. She runs, cradling the box, cradling her dead bird.

Then she returns to the garden near the lake surrounded by mountains. In the garden there is a cedar tree, the millenial tree of the country of E., whom she has not forgotten. She digs and digs a hole, as she weeps. She puts the box into the hole which she waters with her tears and she covers it with earth. She murmurs quite softly:

—One day I shall return. You shall see, one day I shall return.